Wolf Magic

Book 2: Coastal Wolves

Printed in the United States of America: First Printing, 2023.

ISBN: 978-1-959981-12-1 (eBook)
ISBN: 978-1-959981-11-4 (paperback)

http://www.hannahwillow217.wordpress.com

Copy/Line Editor: Angela Grimes
Editor: Weslee Imrisek
Formatting: Huckleberry Rahr
Cover Art: Getcovers.com

Coastal Wolves:

1: Pacific Pack

2: Wolf Magic

3: Campus Prowl

4: Loan Wolf

5: Pack Triage

6: Mystical Science

7: Lupine Investigation

Dedication:

As always, I couldn't get this book done without the help of a crew of people. I thank my son for always having great ideas for the overall story line. He puts up with a bunch of PG questions. Wes and Angela take a jumble of words and make magic, better than any witch I know. Vivienne Ironwood jumped in and made sure my wolves stayed in line, a scary job indeed! With the number of books I'm juggling, I am blessed with a group of friends and fellow authors who jump in to help me.

Chapter 1 - There's an App for That
Maria

"We're going to be late!" Maria paced back and forth in the living room, waiting for Georgette. That woman would be the end of both their jobs.

"Stop being such a worrywart. We have at least five minutes. Is there coffee?" Her voice floated down the stairs from where she was getting ready in her room.

Grumbling, Maria headed to the kitchen to pour two travel mugs of the steamy brew. Her stomach grumbled, so she decided to grab a couple of oat muffins.

"Hurry up, slowpoke, we're going to be late!" Georgette ran past her with a grin, brown hair flying, aimed for the garage.

Maria snarled under her breath, snagged the coffee and muffins, then followed her packmate. In the garage, she slid into the passenger seat of Georgette's blue Subaru Forester, and handed the aggravating woman her coffee. If she weren't Maria's best friend ...

Georgette sipped the coffee. "Oh! Orin made it this morning."

Cupping the mug in her hands, Maria took a deep sniff of the dark brew. Orin's morning offerings were always richer and more satisfying. He kept to himself the secret of creating something better from the same beans everyone else used, though the two had been pestering him about it for years.

After her first sip, Maria moaned in appreciation. "I wonder what got him up so early. He hasn't made coffee during the week in forever."

"Maybe he's just happy Vernon and Steve are gone. I know I am." Georgette swung into the parking lot of Digital iTech. "Even though Tamsin and Paige just left for Chicago and they'll be away for awhile. I get giddy every time I think about her as our new alpha. I'm so excited knowing we have her back in the fold, aren't you?"

Maria took a moment to let the joy of having a new alpha flow through her. "Of course I am. Just imagine it; maybe the rest of the pack will return."

"Maybe, but some of the old pack members ended up getting better jobs in their new cities. I don't know that they'll want to return. We'll have to build our pack the old fashion way." Georgette snapped her teeth at Maria, then winked.

"If anyone can do it, Tamsin can ... without resorting to biting people. Her whole family has a great reputation."

Georgette rolled her eyes, then pulled into a parking spot. "Her family *did* have an excellent reputation, but she ran from it. Don't think wolves won't take that into consideration. Our pack isn't going to grow fast. I mean, we're in an excellent location, but beyond that, Tamsin will have to prove herself."

Maria smirked at her friend. "What about you? Why don't you find a nice mate? Someone to bring to the pack?"

Georgette laughed, throwing her head back as she released her amusement. "You know I have no plans on dating anyone. I'm happy being part of the pack, and do hope we get little ones again some day, but as for finding someone ... no. That's not me, and you know it."

Maria opened the door. Digital iTech was a four-story building supporting designers, developers, project managers, and marketers. If someone wanted something created in the IT world, their company could do it.

The atrium opened up to all four stories of the building in a beautiful feat of architecture. The ceiling skylights allowed guests to see the bright blue California sky. Crossing the open entrance to the elevators, Maria and Georgette punched in the third floor.

"You know, Maria, you *should* think about dating. You stopped when Vernon began making noises of taking over a couple of years ago. Unlike me, you *do* want someone in your life."

Maria rubbed her temples. "That's easier said than done. I wouldn't know where to start, and even if I found someone, how do we explain all of this?" She waved her hands up and down taking in both their bodies.

Georgette laughed. "You do know that our kind have been dating and mating for years. It *is* possible. Since bar hopping has never been your thing ... you *could* go to the beach. Hang out with Paige when she gets back. *Or,* you know, try a dating app. We do work in tech; you shouldn't be afraid of an app."

The elevator doors opened and they walked down a well lit hallway with a Mardi Gras theme. Murals, paintings, and sculptures put the floor in a mood for a King Cake every day. Or maybe that was just Maria.

Georgette followed her into her office, shutting the door behind her. "I'm serious, you should at least try one of the apps. You haven't been out in too long. If you started dating you'd at least work out your kinks."

"Are you calling me kinky?"

"Well, if the paw fits ... but no, it's been awhile, my friend. Go out, learn how to date. You never know, maybe you really will find someone."

Maria's head hit her desk. She heard some ruffling sounds. When she peeked, Georgette sat on the corner of her desk, purse next to her hip, with Maria's phone in her hand. Blue eyes glinting, she waggled her eyebrows. "There you go, all done. I've downloaded the app. Now, are you going to set it up, or do I need to do that as well?"

"Wait, what?"

A few minutes of silence, and then: "All set up."

Dread hit Maria's stomach like a bolder. "What did you do?" She reached for her phone. "Give me my phone. Go, get some work done, I'll see you at lunch."

The sound of her door closing behind Georgette had more of a finality than she liked.

She gazed at the app. *Profile photo ...*

Chapter 2 - I Kissed a Girl, For The First Time
Blake

Chey turned into the parking lot of *Girls Unlimited* and pulled into a stall. "I'll be back at three, but I really think you should call in sick, Blake. The weather is awful."

Blake leaned over and kissed her friend's rosy cheek. "Thanks, Mom. I know the weather said snow, but it also said only an inch or two. I'll be fine."

"I know, and being from Minnesota, we should be made of sterner stuff ... I should be made from tougher stuff. But between the cold weather and the crazies ... just stay safe. Have fun dancing." Chey's blue eyes sparkled. "We have a coven meeting tomorrow night. You aren't working then, are you?"

Blake sighed, looking out the window up at the stars and the waning moon. A few clouds were rolling in, but she could still see the moon in all its magnificence. In a week, its beauty would all but disappear from the night's sky. "I don't. Taking Saturday off hurts, though. There's big money to be made, dancing the pole."

Chey shrugged. "I didn't call the meeting; you know that. Take it up with our fearless leader. Now, go. You don't want to be late."

Sliding out of the car, Blake took her bag, and headed into the establishment. Inside, she waved at some of the other women already working the floor.

She weaved her way to the back changing room. Once there, she stripped down until all she wore was her black bra with silver studs and a G-string. She slipped on thigh-high black stockings and a garter belt. In her locker, she found what she used for a skirt. Attached to a black leather belt was a collection of thin, bejeweled, black leather strips that hung down just low enough to cover her undies. When she moved, nothing stayed covered. She thought of it as her peek-a-boo skirt, and it was a crowd favorite.

Over the skirt she added a second belt, her working belt, with a satchel she used to hold money.

Another girl came in while Blake sat in front of the mirror checking her hair and makeup. Blake's blond hair, indicative of so many of the Midwesterners with Norwegian heritage, was curled and hung past her shoulders. It had taken an act of will to get her hair to curl. She applied a smoky eyeshadow to bring out the blue of her eyes and blood-red lipstick. This wasn't a look for out in public, but that wasn't her job tonight. She added a light blue glitter to her cheek bones.

This is as good as it gets. Blake slipped on the four inch mirrored black heels, and headed out to the floor.

Julie, her manager, came up to her. "You'll be on the floor until one, then you have the stage. You have the stage again at two. Three of your regulars have already requested a lap dance."

Blake smiled and nodded. The regulars, who requested the lap dances, was where she could really make her money. She didn't love this job, but she was good at it, and it paid well.

She dreamed of starting her own nursery one day, and that took money. She'd always been good with growing plants, and this was the start of her dream. The second part was starting an apothecary. She was good with spells and creating tinctures. The magic parts of the business would all have to be on the down low. She knew, once she had her business, late nights dancing to earn her money would be worth it.

She headed over to the tables in her area to take drink orders. A hand grabbed her ass. She turned to give the man a piece of her mind—

there was no touching without paying—and saw a cute brunette woman with a *Bride to Be* tiara.

The woman was petite and pretty with curves in all the right places, very much Blake's type. She was a bit young, but play was play. With a smirk, Blake straddled the woman, wrapping her arms around her neck. "Hey, sexy; I hear tonight's your night. Who's the lucky man ... or woman? Are they here? Or do I have free reign to kiss the bride?"

Her friends went wild, whooping and screaming. The woman froze under Blake, her brown eyes wide and her mouth open in a small O of surprise. "My fiancé isn't here. He's off with his friends somewhere." She gaped at her friends, then back at Blake. "You want to kiss me?"

One of her friends stuffed something in Blake's waistband. "Turn her gay! Show her what a kiss should be."

Blake shimmied up the woman's lap, her smile widening. "What do you say, bride-to-be? Do you wanna be kissed?" Blake licked her top lip slowly.

The woman's tongue shot out, licking her own lips as she nodded. Blake took the woman's hands and placed them on her sides, then slid her own hands behind the bride-to-be's head as she slowly leaned in. Their mouths met and Blake traced her lips with her tongue. When the woman moaned, Blake leaned forward and deepened the kiss. She tasted of tequila and citrus.

Cool fingers dug into Blake's back, and the woman took a choppy breath through her nose. Chuckling, Blake pulled back. "Congratulations, lucky lady." She let her hands slide down the woman's front, smirking at the hard nipples under the tiny dress she wore.

One of the women at the table handed Blake a thin stack of bills. "That was excellent. She needs to learn how to loosen up."

Blake secured the money in her small satchel, curtseyed to the table, and headed to her section to start taking orders. This was the start of a good night.

CHAPTER 3 - WITH TWO BUCKETS AND A BROOM, OBVIOUSLY!
Tamsin

Tamsin had only been back in Chicago a few days, and the city was welcoming her with snow. Lots and lots of snow.

Paige stared out the window of the Bucktown Irish pub they chose for dinner. They'd each ordered the specialty of the night, bangers and mash, and a local brew. Paige's mouth fell open as the snowflakes fell. "It's so pretty, it's like stars falling to the ground ... a lot of stars ... and cold."

"I'm guessing it's colder up in space." She gazed at Paige, the beautiful woman who had followed her to Chicago. *Has she even seen snow before?*

"Okay, all the things that need to happen while we're living in Chicago."

Paige's focus kept darting to the evil white devil flakes falling from the sky. Tamsin shook her head at Paige's folly. *Well, once we move to Santa Cruz at the end of the school year, snow will be a thing of the past.*

Tamsin sighed. "I need to throw you in the Green Lake."

Paige nodded. "Yeah, that sounds great."

"Paige, love, I know you're distracted, but can we get through this list?"

"But Tam ... snow. Like, oh my gods, snow." She started bouncing. "It's fantastic!"

"After dinner, okay?" Tamsin smiled. This woman! "List of things first."

"Right, list ... did you threaten to throw me in green water?"

Tamsin laughed, the mirth bubbling up from her gut. "Okay, I need to call all of the former members of the Pacific Pack. Now that Vernon is gone, maybe we can bring some of them back."

"Can I help with that?"

A growl erupted from Tamsin before she could stop it. "I'm sorry, love, but no. I need to do this. The wolves, they know me. And as alpha, I need to talk to them. I need to explain why it took me so long."

Paige slumped. "Fine, I'm just going to be bored until I figure out someone to write for. Maybe I can get back to my book. The kraken came from beneath ... wait, are there kraken?"

"No!" Tamsin snorted. Then she tilted her head, contemplating the question. "No, I'm pretty sure the answer is no. You can help me by searching for teaching jobs in the greater Santa Cruz area. I need to start applying. It may already be too late. Though, I need to quit, and if there are others like me quitting this late in the season, maybe it isn't too late." She massaged her temples.

Paige ate some of her dinner, then sipped her beer. "Is that it? That list didn't sound so bad."

"Of course not, oh optimistic one. I need to contact all of the alphas. There are seven major packs in the U.S. I need to contact each of the pack leaders and let them know of the shift in leadership. I also want us to stay off the Chicago pack's radar as long as possible. I'll call the alpha, just not yet. I've hidden my power level from them for years ... I guess I'll have to let them know now."

Paige yanked her eyes from the window and smiled at Tamsin. "You think?" Her gaze wandered back to the window. "Wow! The snow is distracting. It's amazing. Isn't April late in the season for snow?"

Tamsin leaned back in the sturdy wooden chair. The low lights and welcoming ambiance of the restaurant warmed her soul. The music drowned out the talk from the other tables, and it somehow felt like they were the only two there, despite the full restaurant. "It is, but it isn't unheard of. I'm just glad it's happening on a Friday night. The roads are going to suck and with a few weeks of no snow before this, everyone has probably forgotten how to drive."

Paige's brow furrowed. "The driving gets that much worse?"

Tamsin snorted. "You are adorable. Yes. Let's finish our dinners and go play."

Bellies full, they headed out to a local forest preserve Tamsin knew about where they could run as wolves.

As Tamsin drove, Paige flipped through her phone. "The weather report says we shouldn't get more than an inch of snow. The car was rock solid as we drove out here, but there were two cars in the ditch already. Should we just head home?"

"How often will you get to run in the snow? We're heading back to California once the school year's done." Out of the car, Tamsin pulled the woman who'd changed her life into her arms for a deep kiss. She still couldn't believe this change in her solitary life.

They quickly stripped, folding their clothes and stashing them in the car, then began their shift to wolves. Tamsin made sure Paige started before she found her own wolf.

The shift didn't take long, and once Tamsin was on four paws, she turned until she found the white wolf with black shading on her ears, tails, and paws. She loved how Paige looked in both forms.

The area they chose wasn't large, but they just wanted to frolic for a few hours while the snow speckled the sky. They played tag, chasing each other. When Tamsin caught Paige, she tackled the other wolf. In retaliation, Paige pushed her black snout down to sniff at Tamsin's neck as she playfully pretended to attack any sensitive area she could find.

Finding her paws, Tamsin was about to dart off when it occurred to her the snow was almost up to her knees. This was no 'one inch of snow.' With an irritated snuffle, she turned towards the car at a trot. Paige followed.

They quickly found their humanity—and scrambled into their clothes, then got into the heated car.

Paige noted what Tamsin had already figured out. "This isn't a small snowstorm, is it? This is way more than an inch."

"We need to get home; good thing I pay for a parking spot."

As they neared their neighborhood, chairs with brooms littered the street. Paige eyed the odd paraphernalia. Her brows came together, and her forehead wrinkled. Her head started whipping back and forth. "What's going on?"

Tamsin snorted. "As people clear a spot, they 'reserve' it with whatever they have on hand so other people know it's no longer up for grabs."

"But ... it's street parking, right?"

"Yes, but those people cleared the snow. They didn't do it for just anybody."

"But it's public parking. How do you claim it?"

Tamsin lifted a brow. "With two buckets and a broom, obviously."

The next morning, Tamsin slipped out of bed and padded to the bathroom. She gazed out at the world blanketed in white. It was spectacular. Most of the beauty lay in knowing they didn't have anywhere to go. After washing her hands, she headed to the kitchen to start the coffee maker. The lock screen of her phone had a city-wide warning asking residents to stay in. Tapping on the message, she read that the overnight blizzard dropped over sixteen inches of snow in the greater Chicagoland area. Some areas of the upper Midwest got over two feet.

Tamsin placed her phone on the counter and dug in the refrigerator for eggs and bacon. Smiling slyly, she realized she had an entire day to play with Paige ... now, to convince her lover that clothes weren't necessary if the heat in the apartment was high enough.

CHAPTER 4 - WHO KNOWS HOW TO MEASURE ANYWAY?
Blake

The blaring of the alarm matched the throbbing in Blake's head. She shouldn't have accepted all the drinks last night, but when she drank with the customers, they tipped her more.

With a groan, she slammed her fist onto the boxy clock—manufactured in the previous century—then rolled onto her back and rubbed her temples. A small whimper escaped as a drummer took up residency in her head.

She checked the clock and saw she had to get up. Chey would be here to take her to the coven meeting in less than an hour and she needed to shower and eat ... and take something to knock out the drummer.

It took some maneuvering, but she managed to drag herself from bed. She trudged to the kitchen and got the coffee started. A glass of water with some medicine was next and then to the bathroom. She started the shower, turning the water to a bit warmer than usual. The hot water was a balm to her soul.

She didn't give herself as much time as she would have liked under the beating streams of hellfire water. She'd splurged and bought a massage head for her shower, to help destress after a night of work, but she didn't have time to utilize its magic before the meeting. The jets massaged her shoulders and neck in waves of bliss but pick up was happening soon.

Once out of the shower, she pulled on a set of thermal pants and a thermal shirt before her jeans, a turtleneck, and a sweater. Digging in her drawer, she found warm woolen socks. Back in the kitchen, she poured herself a large amount of go-go-juice. Once she had her mug of black coffee, she finally braved a look out the window and saw the world was blanketed in a layer of white.

Didn't the weather report say one inch?

Everything outside her tiny apartment lost definition. The parking lot full of cars looked like a sea with tiny bumps that could be rocks, or turtles. The large pine trees looked like holiday cookies come to life. No distinction existed between the sidewalk, road, and lawns. It was as if someone decided everything needed a redo, and whitewashed the city.

Blake growled low in her throat as she sipped her dark brew, letting the caffeine do its worst. Gazing at the world turned snowscape made her insides shiver. With a final glare, she turned from the sight and dug in the cupboard for bagels. She popped one in the toaster. Once it was out, she added cream cheese, and sat to eat.

While she broke her fast, she finally checked her phone.

On the lock screen, an advisory popped up to inform her that a freak blizzard had blown through all of the Midwest dumping sixteen to twenty-four inches of snow. *'Unless an emergency, all residents are asked to stay indoors for the next twenty-four hours while city officials work to clear roads.'*

Opening her phone, Blake checked her messages. Sure enough, she had a message from Chey. `Hey, the meeting tonight has been canceled. Stay in, be safe. I know you like going out, even in bad weather, but for my sake, don't.`

Blake smiled. Chey was always worrying over her. `There's over two feet of snow out there. Why would I leave my apartment? I think I'm beginning to hate snow!`

Though her text to her friend was a joke, as she gazed at the words, she began to think about them. Why *did* she still live in a state that had blizzards in April? She could move somewhere warm, like Florida or Texas. Florida scared her;

she'd heard a lot of stories about Florida Man and the crazy things he did. Texas made her a bit nervous too; she preferred dating women, and she wasn't exactly sure how accepting the state was. But there were other states that didn't have this much snow.

Her mom had moved after her dad had died. The only thing keeping her here was the coven. Was that really enough? She could start a nursery anywhere.

Well, she hadn't had enough coffee to really think about this now. She should spend her free day studying some new coven spells. It was rare for her to have the night off. *That's it, it's decided: movie, ice cream, pajamas, and a fuzzy blanket!*

CHAPTER 5 - IF YOU WANT TO DATE, MAKE YOUR OWN PROFILE
Maria

Everyone in the pack—all four of them—sat in the backyard, enjoying the nice Sunday weather. Maria gazed at her mimosa and shook her head with a smile. *Connie and her morning drinks! Well, Connie hadn't felt like mixing morning mimosas since*

Vernon had taken over months before ... it is nice having the old pack back ... even if it is smaller.

It had been a week since they'd seen off their fearless leader and her new love. Even without Tamsin in residence, everything felt ... better.

Orin stood. "Anyone else need more to drink? Maybe coffee this time?" His blond hair and brown eyes made him look like a surfer. Having lived most of his life in Santa Cruz, he looked much younger than his forty-three years. So did his wife, Connie. She was three years older than him, but they both looked to be in their early thirties, at most.

Connie grunted. "Last night at the restaurant was a doozie. Some group came in for a twenty-first birthday celebration. I don't know why they didn't just go to your average bar, but they stayed until close ordering food all night. The kitchen could barely keep up. I guess coffee would be a good follow-up ... fine."

Maria leaned back and sighed, letting the warmth of the sun heat her up. "If you're making it, I'll take some, too."

Georgette punched her shoulder. "Did you hear that Maria here has a date tonight?"

Maria groaned. "I was hoping to not think about that until the afternoon. Can't we all just enjoy the morning?"

Connie shot up to sitting, leaning on her knees. "You have a date? It's been years! Spill, girl."

Her only response was to throw her arm over her eyes.

A traitor to the end, Georgette laughed. "I made her join a dating app, and her first date is tonight.

Maria felt her blanket shift and peeked under her arm. "Are you really going through my phone?"

"How else will we get the details?" Georgette asked. "Let's see, tonight's date is with a man named 'John.'"

Maria reached up and snatched her phone. "Gods above, you're incorrigible. Again, if you want to date, make your own profile."

"Nope, just want to tease you. Now, a guy?"

"I'm just testing the waters. My last girlfriend ... the relationship didn't end well." Maria squeezed her eyes shut. She both loved and hated how close the pack was. "Now, can we literally talk about anything else?"

Before anyone could respond, her phone rang. She answered without even checking who called. She didn't care if it were a telemarketer or a serial killer. Anything was better than the current conversation. "Hello?"

"Hi? Maria? Is that you?"

Rolling her head back, she tried to place what she heard. She knew the voice. Next to her, Georgette whispered, "Holy hells, is that Tory Byrd?"

Maria shot up to sitting, clutching the phone to her ear. "Tory? Is that you?"

A soft chuckle came over the line. "I knew you'd remember me! Yeah, it's Tory."

"Hey, what's up?"

"Well, I don't know a good way to say this, but I hear that Tamsin is back and she got rid of Tweedle Dumb and Tweedle Dumber, the evil version."

A warmth infused Maria. It was happening: their old pack had heard that Vernon and Steve were gone, and maybe, just maybe, they'd come back. She knew she was putting the horse before the cart, but she hoped that was what this call was about.

"Yeah, you heard right. Vernon and Steve are gone. Actually, so is Tamsin, but not for long. Once her school year is over, she's moving back and taking over."

"That's amazing. I was ... well ... I don't know what things are like out there now, but do you have room in the pack house for tiny me? I moved to Texas and joined their pack. I mean, it isn't awful, but I see how Vernon came from here, and why he left. I'd like to come home."

"We'd love to have you. Tory, we really would."

Once Maria finished the call, she called Tamsin to tell her the good news.

"That's fantastic," the new alpha enthused. "The pack bonds will strengthen with each return, each addition."

Maria bit her lip. "Have you made any of the calls yet?"

There was a pause, before Tamsin sighed. "We flew in last Sunday and had to get everything set up and me back to work on Monday. I've been playing catchup at school all week. Then, yesterday, the whole Midwest was hit by a freak blizzard. Paige has never seen snow, so we took some time to enjoy ourselves."

From beside her, Connie grinned. "You know, if the two of you are ... ah ... busy, I could make the calls. My days are free anyway."

A small growl came over the line, and Maria could feel a bit of frustration through the pack bonds. That was new; the bonds had been held closed for so long, she forgot what it was to feel anything through them. All four of the wolves in the backyard perked up at the sensation, despite the emotion being negative.

Connie snorted. "Fine, fine. Alpha's prerogative, got it. I won't step on your toes, Tamsin. We can't wait to see you back home."

Maria was supposed to meet her date, John, at a New Orleans restaurant. After debating on what to wear for way too long, she'd slipped on a fitted mauve dress with ballerina flats and a black shawl. She pinned her shoulder-length black waves up on the sides and called it good enough.

John met her outside of Café Étouffée. He wore light gray slacks and a blue polo shirt. The blue of the shirt brought out his eyes. His hair was neat and trim. Her first impression was ... pleasant, he looked pleasant. She was sure they'd have a wonderful time at dinner.

The two went in and were seated in the window seat. Their waiter, Kenny, a tall man with long dreadlocks, immediately became their best friend. He had moved to Santa Cruz from New Orleans a few years back and Maria could tell this man made the restaurant.

After speaking with Kenny for a few minutes, they ended up with a sample platter: a half shrimp po'boy sandwich each, small cups of étouffée, jambalaya, gumbo, and beignets for dessert.

The meal was divine. The date ... not so much. John spoke about investing money and the stock market the whole time. He never once asked Maria about herself.

When the beignets came, he smiled up at her. "These are amazing! How much of this meal do you think you could cook? Or do you mainly cook Mexican food?"

Maria's brows furrowed, as she looked at John, confused. "Mexican food? Cook? What do you think I do for a living, John? I mean, you've spent the evening speaking about yourself and your work, but ... what is it you think this is?"

He sat back, eyes wide, as if he hadn't thought she could speak. "Well, I don't know. Your profile doesn't say much about what you do, I kind of thought you were either looking for a hookup or were old fashioned, you know, and your outfit definitely doesn't say 'hookup.' I figured you wanted to stay at home and cook and clean. I mean, I make enough, that's what I've been trying to tell you. I get that we need to know each other better before we move forward with any arrangement, but you're pretty enough for me."

Maria just gaped at the man, slack-jawed. She hadn't really paid much attention to the profile Georgette had set up, but she was fairly certain her best friend would've put in a job, especially since they worked together. Forcibly shutting her mouth, she smiled. "Hold on." And waved a finger at him ... her pointer finger, though she debated using the middle one for a second.

She pulled out her phone, and opened the dating app. Going through the profile, she searched for the different details. Under occupation, it said: IT. Maria rolled her eyes, and held her phone out to John. "You do know what 'IT' is, don't you, John?"

"Well, yes. I just sorta figured you didn't."

Maria snatched her purse, stood up, and walked out of the restaurant.

CHAPTER 6 - A FINAL GOOD-BYE
Blake

"Will there be anything else, pretty ladies?"

Blake smiled at the bartender, then shook her head. "This should be good for now, thanks."

She picked up her glass of wine, and held it up to her two best friends. "Here's to the triple threat."

Chey sighed. "I don't like this. You want to toast, but you plan on leaving, Blake. I can't believe it."

"Why not? Dad died a few years ago, and Mom moved away, not that she was even a witch. The coven and you two are all I have here, and the snow is awful. I want to go somewhere it doesn't hurt to breathe."

They all sipped their wine, and Blake leaned back, content.

Gretel, the youngest of the coven at twenty-one, narrowed her eyes. "Have you figured out where you're going to go?"

"That I have, my friend." Blake lifted her glass in salute. "My aunt, Cinthia, is a coven leader in Santa Cruz. I called her last night and she said she'd love to have me join. I'm still debating."

With a sharp intake of air, Gretel gaped at her. "Are you for real? Santa Cruz?"

"Yeah, why?"

"Because that's one of the dental hygienist schools I got into ... it's right outside of Santa

Cruz. The waiting list to get into these programs takes forever. I kinda had the same thinking you did: get away from the snow, see the ocean. Chey's mom told me there was a coven out there. I thought, why not? I start in June ... I didn't know how to tell you two." She bit her lower lip. "If I'd gotten into a closer program ... but I didn't."

Blake's heart pounded faster. "You mean, maybe we could move out there together?"

Chey groaned. "Really? You're *both* leaving me?"

Gretel smiled mischievously. "You could come with us."

"No, I can't. You know I can't. My mom runs the coven, and I'm slated to take over for her. Losing two members is going to rock the coven as it is, losing a third—and the eventual witch who is supposed to take over—that would be too much, and you both know it."

Gretel looked down at her hands. Chey had never picked up on Gretel's attraction. Chey never picked up on anyone's attraction. That woman was oblivious. With her big blue eyes and flowing blond hair, she was a knockout, but she obviously never got the memo. Gretel was tall and lean, with flirty short brown hair and brown eyes. Blake would happily have taken her out to the strip club and found her some action, but she really only had eyes for one person. Leaving Minnesota would either be heartbreaking for the girl, or the perfect solution.

It took them a week to arrange subletters for their apartments, quit their jobs, pack up all their stuff into a large moving van—neither of them had much—and say their goodbyes to the coven.

The night before they left, the coven made a circle under the new moon. Pulling the energy from the four cardinal directions, they performed a spell of goodbye and safe travel.

Chey took the pinnacle position. "Hecate, watch over our sisters as they take this journey." The women in the circle, including Blake and Gretel, scooped their arms out, over their head, and down, ending with their palms together in front of their hearts.

Gazing at the center, Chey demanded, "Safety!"

All the women snapped their hands towards the center, palms up. Colors danced above all the palms, representing their powers and proficiencies.

The rainbow of colors coming from the women showed the strength of the coven, something that always brought pride to Blake's soul. Each woman around her had two brilliant colors blazing from their hands. With a sigh, Blake gazed at the two green flames coming from her. As a half-witch, she'd be the weakest link in any coven, unable to do what a full witch like Chey, or even Gretel, could do.

"We will miss you, Blake and Gretel, as you move your life out west. If your life brings you back here, know you always have a place in our coven."

Everyone rolled their fingers in, making fists and extinguishing their flames. Though Blake wanted this, the finality of the motion felt a bit like a punch to her chest. A tear trailed down her cheek as she searched the faces around the circle for the last time. Each member smiled back warmly, emanating peace, hope, and joy.

The next morning, she and Gretel trudged to the truck as early as they could drag themselves from bed and began the drive west.

CHAPTER 7 - YOU WANT TO KILL ME?
Tamsin

"How was your day?"

"Good? And yours?" Tamsin threw her gym bag in the trunk of her car and stared blankly at it. She'd been slowly explaining to her clients that there was an end date for their workouts. She'd been back in Chicago just over a month, and in another month, she'd leave again. She didn't know if she'd be back.

"Great. I've submitted two more articles for Dominik. He doesn't like that I'm not available for local stories, but he's happy with what I'm writing." Paige was a journalist for the Daily Cruz in Santa Cruz. They'd never hired her full-time, so her taking a couple of months to live in Chicago with Tamsin shouldn't put too much of a damper on her ability to work for them. "So, are you going to finally do it?"

Tamsin snarled.

"That's very impressive, Tam, but that doesn't answer my question."

"Fine. Yes, I told him I'd come today, and I will."

"I don't know why you've been putting it off."

Tamsin sighed. "Look, when I see Nolan, I'm going to have to tell him everything. Explain to him who I am, who you are, and that I lied to him about who I was for all those years. He's not going to like that. And then, on top of that, I'm going to explain that I'm the new alpha of the Santa Cruz pack, stronger than his alpha, and staying for the next full moon. You can guess how well *that's* going to go over."

"Oh ... yeah. I guess I hadn't really thought about all that." She paused, then snorted. "Have fun!"

"You're sadistic, you know that."

"Good thing you love me. Now, if you want, I could cook dinner while you're out."

"Oh, gods above, you want to kill me, don't you!"

She laughed, and Tamsin ended the call. She loved Paige, but the woman couldn't cook without supervision. They'd learned that even *with* supervision she could sometimes mess up the recipe. But it was fun playing together in the kitchen, even with the risks.

It didn't take long to get to the gym, or to change, or to find Nolan, already warming up on a bike. Tamsin slid onto the machine next to him after adjusting the settings, and began her warm-up.

He smiled wide. "Hey, stranger. It's been too long. How've you been?"

Tamsin's shoulders dropped. She'd missed her friend. "I've been good, really good."

"Didn't you leave because your aunt died?"

"Yes, but ... gods, so much has happened beyond that one thing ... I don't even know where to start." She gave him a sheepish smile.

Nolan shifted his focus to her. "How about start with, 'Hey Nolan, I met this beautiful woman in Santa Cruz and brought her back with me.'"

Tamsin's mouth dropped open. "You know about Paige?"

He threw his head back and laughed. "Well, I do now, and it's nice to know she has a name." He upped the resistance on his bike. "One of the pack saw you two at a restaurant and I pieced the rest of it together."

"Well, let's just say there was a ... member ... of the Santa Cruz crew who was starting to deteriorate. He had ... harmed ... a tourist, fatally, and Paige ... not fatally. She didn't know what membership meant before he, let's say, took a bite out of journalism."

Nolan's head whipped around and his eyes almost glowed. "Please tell me he's been taken care   of."
"He has."

They moved to the weights, and Tamsin realized the section was completely empty of anyone but them. She'd noticed the gym had been pretty quiet; four o'clock on a Thursday was never a very popular time, but this was crazy slow.

"Has the gym been struggling?" It was owned by one of the pack members, so Nolan would probably know.

Nolan shook his head. "No, this is just a weird lull."

Tamsin nodded. "Okay, good. Twenty-five pound weights. We're going to do routine four today, because it's your least favorite, and I'm guessing you skipped it while I was gone."

Nolan's face broke out in a huge grin. "You know me so well."

Tamsin found a set of eighteen-pound weights, and the two began a series of squats, lunges, high-knee raises, reverse sit ups, burpees, and planks.

Once they'd started their first circuit, Tamsin continued their conversation. "As for Steve, the crazy one, and Vernon, the leader, neither of them survived."

With a quick shake of his head, Nolan panted out, "Who took care of it? They'd have to have someone strong enough to take out ...

leader. And is there a new ... you know ... leader?"

"Nolan, you know my name is Tamsin, you've always known that, but do you know my last name?"

Nolan put the weights away, snatching his water bottle from the floor for a long pull. "Um, well, no, I don't think so. I was just told your name was Tamsin and I was your contact while you lived here. I don't know why I never thought about it."

"Your alpha probably told you not to worry."

"Why? What *is* your last name?"

Tamsin held out her hand. "Nolan Barns, it's a pleasure to meet you, my name is Tamsin Hath."

His mouth fell open. "You're a Hath? How did I not know this? So ... are you leaving? Will you take over your family's pack?"

Tamsin nodded. "Yeah, I'm finally taking my rightful place in Santa Cruz. Vernon did everything he could to mess it up. I need to go back and fix it ... but I need to finish the school year here first."

He glanced around the gym, then leaned closer. "Does my alpha know?"

"Not yet. I've been calling the old pack members and alphas. I was saving the best for last."

Nolan's eyes narrowed. "You'll call him, right? Like, tonight."

Tamsin nodded. "Yes, that's the plan."

CHAPTER 8 - THE WINE HELPED
Maria

Maria sat at her desk at work, scrolling through the dating app. She was going on her second date after work ... on a Monday. She'd put off this second attempt for almost a month after the utter debacle of a first date. She wasn't sure if it was her, John, the fact that he *was* a John—a man—

or what. All she knew was she needed time to lick her wounds.

She went back to Rose's profile. Her date for tonight, Rose had curly brown hair that looked like it bounced when the woman laughed ... she also appeared to laugh a lot, with the wide smile, and laugh lines around her mouth. Her green eyes sparkled in the picture. Unlike most of the other profile pictures, Maria couldn't help smiling back.

Maria had a better feeling about Rose than John. In her profile, Rose said she was forty-three, recently divorced, and looking to get back out into the dating world. She'd first messaged Maria a week ago. All of the people had messaged her first. Maria wasn't ready to make the first digital move.

Scrolling past Rose's profile, she got to Skyler, her date for Friday. She couldn't believe Georgette and Orin had convinced her to make two dates in one week. Well, she had to admit the wine helped. They'd been drinking Saturday night and they'd gotten enough in her that Georgette convinced her to bring her phone out. Things had taken a turn for the worst after that.

Skyler was younger than her thirty-six. A baby of twenty-nine. Maria wasn't sure how she felt about that, but the other two said anyone over the age of twenty-six should be considered datable. "Age plus or minus ten," Orin had said with authority.

The woman had short red hair and piercing green eyes. She wore a bikini in her profile picture. Maria would've never initiated contact with such a spitfire-looking woman, but she did make her heart skip a beat.

Georgette winked. "You know, as wolves, we age a bit slower. Not a lot, but if we play our cards right, we live longer than the average human. With our bodies healing themselves ... good health means a longer life. A younger mate is fine."

Maria shut her phone and faced her computer. She needed to get back to work. She had an hour left and a bit more stuff that really should get done before she left for the day.

Checking herself out in the mirror, Maria sighed. It was as good as it would ever get. Her black hair was pulled up on the sides in sparkling bobby pins. She wore subtle makeup. After spending time sorting through her sundresses, she selected a cerulean blue that was fitted on top and flared down to the tops of her knees. When she bought the dress, she'd also purchased matching sandals.

Once done, she headed down to the main floor of the pack house, only to hear a knock on the door. She wasn't expecting anyone, and she and Rose had agreed to meet at a local sushi restaurant.

As she headed towards the door, she saw Orin come out of the kitchen. Georgette was up in her room, and Connie was already at the restaurant, working.

Maria looked out the peep hole and saw a head of black hair with blue highlights. With a squawk, she pulled open the door. "Tory!" She pulled the other woman into a huge hug. "You're here! You made it!"

Tory laughed. "I told you I was coming."

"Yes, but you didn't say when you'd make it. And you cut it so close to the full moon! It's tomorrow."

Tory's brow rose. "I know it's tomorrow, that's why I made sure to get in by today, silly. Now, let me in. Can I have my old room?"

Orin came up behind them, pulling Tory into a hug. "Of course, sweetie. We've missed you."

She smiled up at him before grabbing her bags and trotting up the stairs.

Orin rubbed Maria's shoulders. "You look lovely, Maria. Go, have fun tonight." He leaned down and kissed her forehead.

With a longing look up the stairs, Maria scrunched up her mouth and nodded. "Yeah, okay, I'll go. I'd rather stay and help welcome Tory. You know, I could message Rose, tell her something came up."

"Maria, go. Tory is moving back, you'll have plenty of time to catch up."

Maria's shoulders slumped as she turned and headed out to the restaurant.

She decided to walk, since the sushi shop was only a few blocks away. She tried to get her head back in the game as she took in the perfect night. A block away from meeting Rose, the sky darkened enough that the street lights popped on. The magical transition from day to night was one of her favorite times of the evening.

Searching the people ahead of her, she saw the taller woman and gave a small wave.

Rose smiled as wide as her profile picture, and waved, her hair bouncing just like Maria thought it would.

The two met in front of the restaurant and shook hands. "Hi, Rose. I'm Maria. Nice to meet you." The other woman towered over her by a few inches.

"Hi! Aren't you just the prettiest thing!"

Maria's eyes widened and she smiled. "Um, thank you."

They entered the restaurant and sat. The waitress delivered their water and menus and gave them time. Maria decided on what she wanted and focused on her date.

Rose met her eyes. "So, I want to make sure you saw on my profile that I've been married and then divorced."

"Yeah, I saw that. I hope it wasn't horrible."

"Oh, it was. He was a pig, and only cared about himself. God, men! Am I right?"

Maria took a sip of her water, wishing it were something stronger. "Oh, you were married to a man?"

The waitress came to take their order before Rose could answer. Once she left, Rose dove in. "Oh, yeah. He was a dick. We married after college. I thought he was my knight in shining armor, but he was just a dud of an ass, if you know what I mean."

Maria gave her a shy smile. "So, you like both men and women, like me. Have you dated many women?"

Rose's brows came together. It was cute, but made Maria worried. "Oh, yeah ... not really. I just wasn't sure if the reason I was never satisfied was because of Chuck being an ass, or because Chuck was a guy." She shrugged, making her hair bounce again. "Anyway, I thought playing with some women may be fun."

Their food came and Maria considered her options. The sushi was as excellent as ever, and the woman across from her was beautiful.

What *were* her goals?

CHAPTER 9 - RAIN! NOT SNOW! I'M HAPPY ALREADY!
Blake

Blake maneuvered the moving van—Matilda, as she'd named the behemoth—into a spot at the cheap hotel. Turning Matilda off, she flopped back in the seat and sighed. Gretel leaned against the door on the passenger side, fast asleep.

Letting her arms hang for a minute, Blake dropped her head against the back of the driver's seat as her body de-stressed from the drive. The last half day's drive through California traffic, tight twisting roads, and distracting scenery almost did her in.

With a grunt, she opened her eyes, and stared at Matilda's stained roof. "Okay, Gretel, time to get up."

The other woman only groaned.

"Gretel." Blake reached over and shook her friend's arm.

One brown eye opened and gazed at her. "Tell me I can get out of this truck and never get back in again."

A smile spread across Blake's face. "Let's get a room, make some phone calls, and figure out this new town we're in."

Gretel pushed herself up with a moan. "Body sore, me tired, brain dead."

"You'll be fine." Blake climbed from the truck. "I'll get you coffee and you'll be right as rain."

"Oh! Rain ... not snow. I'm happy already." How quickly she perked up. *Freaking youth! Doesn't appreciate the beauty of taking time to adjust from being cranky and asleep to chipper and awake!*

They made their way to the front desk of the hotel and got a room. Once they had their bags, they collapsed on the beds, happy to finally be out of the moving truck and in Santa Cruz.

Blake opened her phone and found her aunt's phone number. She wasn't sure if Cinthia would answer. She'd called before leaving Minnesota, but only left a message. She hadn't expected the trip to take so long.

It was mid-May and they'd only just arrived in the coastal city. Between packing, getting out of their apartment leases, selling items they wouldn't need, and saying good-bye to everyone, leaving the Midwest took almost two weeks. The drive took another four days. Now they just needed to find a place they could unpack and call their own.

"Hello? Blake? Did I do this darn cell phone thing right? Gods above, I need to ask one of the kids how to use this darn thing."

"Aunt Cinthia?"

"Blake?"

A warmth infused Blake. She hadn't seen or heard from her aunt in years, but her voice had always been soothing. "Hi, Aunt Cinthia. I finally made it into town. My friend and I just got a hotel room for the night. We're so tired of being in that stupid truck."

"Oh, sweetie, I wish you'd called. You could've stayed here, we have plenty of rooms. How about tomorrow you move in here until you find somewhere else? You could even come now. Forget that room."

"I don't know how good of company we'd be. Gretel is practically asleep right now. I think we're going to just not move for a few hours."

"How about this? It's only eleven in the morning, no matter what time it feels for you. Rest, and come here this afternoon. You'll be happier staying here. The house is nice and we have several rooms. You can unpack and stay for a few days, or longer. We can put your stuff into storage until you find a job and then an apartment."

Blake sighed. "I'll talk to Gretel."

A few hours later, Blake maneuvered Matilda—her nemesis, the moving truck from hell—through side streets that were too small for the behemoth of a moving van. Her hands squeezed the steering wheel until her knuckles were white and she wanted to scream in frustration.

"Breathe, Blake. I think it's just around the next corner." Gretel held her phone up, her eyes bouncing from the road, to her phone, then to Blake.

Biting back a growl, Blake turned where Gretel pointed and saw an old two-story house and knew that had to be it. She could feel the power emanating from the house that had to have been in the family of a witch for years. She could even see some aura colors surrounding the building. The glow was stunning.

She parked Matilda and leapt out ... well, stumbled, and caught herself before she landed on her ass. The sun beat down on her from the clear blue sky as she debated her options for the next few nights. She wanted to head into the house with a plan. The idea of staying in this glowing home appealed to her, but they had to have an escape route. *Mom always taught me to be prepared.*

After thinking things through with her half-addled brain, she followed Gretel up the steps to the door. "Can you imagine these stairs in an area where it snowed?"

Gretel snorted. "It would be awful. So would the roads. These people have no idea. Just the idea of their ignorance makes me giddy ... like, no snow. Doesn't that sound divine?"

After the freak spring blizzard, Blake could only nod and agree.

They knocked on the door and only waited a moment before her aunt answered. Smiling in joy, Aunt Cinthia wrapped her in a hug. "Blake, lovely as always, though you've grown so much! You look so much like your father. I'm so glad you decided to come." She stepped back, then grabbed Gretel's hands. "And you, young lady, must be Gretel. Your old coven leader called, and I'm excited to have both of you here."

She led them into a home much more modern than Blake expected. The open living room, dining room, and kitchen were sleek and welcoming. Aunt Cinthia waved to the stairs. "Those lead to the guest rooms. We can start there, so you two can see where you'll be staying until you find jobs."

Gretel sighed. "That would be wonderful. We've been sleeping in the cab of the moving truck to save money, and the deciding factor to drag ourselves here was how uncomfortable the beds were at that cheap hotel."

"And how dirty everything felt," Blake mumbled.

Aunt Cinthia laughed as she directed them each to a different room. "I just bought this house from the previous owners, so no one is living here yet. There's a master bedroom downstairs with a jacuzzi tub, and one of the rooms up here has an attached bathroom."

Gretel bit her lip. "I think Blake should have first pick. I mean, she *is* your family."

"Yes, but this is the coven's house, not mine."

Blake considered. "Are you specifically trying to keep the master suite downstairs free?"

"Yeah, in case anyone wants to use the tub. It would be awkward if someone were occupying the bedroom."

Nodding, Blake walked to a random door. "I'll take this room."

Aunt Cinthia smiled. "Perfect. The previous owners moved out quickly, so if she left anything, just let me know. Tamsin is in Chicago, but she'll be back in town in a few weeks. I'm sure you'll meet her at some point. She's like family."

Blake shook her head. "You knew the former owner?"

"Well, yes. It's a bit of a story, but the cliffnotes are, Tamsin's aunt and uncle owned the house. They both died. Her aunt was part of the coven. When Tamsin went to sell, we offered to buy. The basement is the perfect place to mix potions; I can't wait for you to see it, except I'd like you both to be a bit more awake first, to appreciate it."

Again, Blake felt lost. "If Tamsin is planning on living in Santa Cruz, why didn't she keep the house?"

"Well, dear, she's the local werewolf pack alpha. She'll need to move into her pack's house."

Blake froze, unable to comprehend the words her aunt had just muttered. Gretel, on the other hand, had no problem. "A wolf? A werewolf used to own this house? You bought a house from a werewolf? That's ..."

"Careful, young one," Aunt Cinthia admonished. "In this city the witches and wolves are friends. In most of the big cities they are. It is only in places where the groups are separate that ignorance brings discord."

Greta's mouth shut with an audible snap. She turned and went into another of the rooms.

Blake watched her, her gut tight with disappointment and hurt. She tried to keep her face blank as she turned to her aunt. "She'll learn and do better; she's still young."

Aunt Cinthia's brow rose. "But not you? You're okay with wolves and witches intermixing?"

"I don't know what I'm okay with right now. I'm still travel-tired."

"Well, take a shower and meet me downstairs for dinner. The rest of the coven should be here shortly to meet you. I know you're tired, but they are so excited to have new meat ... er ... no, that's what I meant, new meat to indoctrinate." She chuckled to herself as she turned and headed towards Gretel's door, knocking before entering.

The room Blake selected was nice, well decorated, and comfortable. She quickly put her bag on the bed, selected a clean outfit and gathered her toiletries, then headed to the bathroom to shower.

Clean and feeling more herself, she knocked on Gretel's door. "If that's Blake, come in."

She slowly opened the door. Gretel lay on the bed on her stomach, reading a book. "You ready to head down to eat?"

Gretel took in a long, slow breath. "I guess. I didn't mean to offend your aunt, I just ... wolves. Blake, can you imagine? I never thought I'd meet one, much less have to socialize with them. I just ... where are we?"

"Do you think it'll be that bad?" Blake walked across the room and sat on the edge of the bed.

"Yes ... no ... I don't know. What if they're mean, and snarl, and want to bite us? Or mate with us? Or, I dunno, what do you think it'll be like?"

"Honestly? I think it'll be like meeting people. You sound like the people who are afraid of meeting witches. In all honesty, you've probably met a werewolf and didn't even know it. They're people, just like we're people. Now, my friend, let's go and meet our new coven."

Blake pulled her friend up and they trudged down the hall to the stairs. She couldn't believe how long the day had already been, and they were starting a whole new part. From the stairs, she could hear talking and laughing coming from the first floor. As they turned the corner to the great room, she saw a room full of people, and she could feel the power from so many witches in one place.

Not everyone had the same abilities, and her ability to feel and see witch-power was rare. She always knew a witch when she met one. She often knew their strength as well. There were a lot of strong witches in the room.

One of the women in the room with long, frizzy, auburn hair jerked when they got to the kitchen. Her vivid green eyes locked on Blake as she made her way over.

Aunt Cinthia, gliding around the kitchen getting people drinks and snacks, smiled at them. "What can I get the two of you?"

Blake smiled. "Whatever you're mixing sounds great."

Aunt Cinthia smiled, grabbed a pitcher, and poured two glasses. Blake took a sip. The cool strawberry margarita tasted divine.

The fiery redhead made it over to them and Aunt Cinthia smiled at her. "Why, Fe, glad you made it over here. Did you want to meet my niece, Blake, and her friend, Gretel? They just drove in from Minnesota and one of the covens there."

Fe narrowed her eyes at Blake. "Cinthia, can you explain to me why you're calling a wolf a witch?"

CHAPTER 10 - YOU KNOW YOU'RE MY FAVORITE
Maria

A shaking woke Maria, and it took her a second to realize a hand on her shoulder was the cause and not an earthquake. She pushed herself up, rubbed her eyes, yawned, and stretched. "What are you doing waking me up at ..." her head flopped to the side trying to make sense of the numbers on the clock, "... stupid o'clock in the morning?"

Before the answer came, she wrapped her blanket tight around herself, making a warm cocoon. She didn't want the cool morning air waking her up unless this really was an emergency. The look in Connie's eyes made her feel she'd be back asleep sooner than later.

"Is that an official time?" Connie's perky voice didn't help the situation. The other woman sat at the end of the bed and rubbed Maria's leg.

"Any time before five is stupid. Now, is there an emergency? You aren't acting like it." A yawn vibrated through her head before she could focus on any answer.

"Tamsin sent a text last night while I was working, asked me to have someone call her between six and seven her time; that's four to five our time. I'm going to bed ... so, I volunteer you, my friend." She spun on her heel and walked out of the room.

Maria pushed herself up to sitting with a groan. Her body buzzed with exhaustion, but she knew if she gave it time, she'd adjust to being awake. Her date had ended late last night;

she'd only gotten a bit of sleep, and tonight was a full moon. "Gah!" She mumbled to herself. *Maybe I'll call in sick. I have plenty of days to take off. I'll call Tam, figure out what's so important, then go back to sleep until our run tonight. Nothing is that pressing at work.*

Lying back down, she dialed Tamsin's number and rolled over so the phone was pressed up to her ear. It only rang a couple of times before her alpha answered. "Maria, are you actually awake? I can't believe Connie woke you up!"

She growled and Tamsin laughed. "This had better be worth my only getting a few hours sleep."

"Why so little? Did you have one of your dates last night? Did it go well?"

She'd have blushed if she had had more sleep. "I'm not calling to gossip, Tam. Why did I call you?"

"Right. Well, apparently Cinthia's niece drove in from Minnesota after the big blizzard last month. She's been a coven witch her whole life, but what she's been hiding from her coven for years, is that she's *also* a wolf."

The shivers of exhaustion mixed with thoughts of doubt and apprehension. "Have we ever heard of someone being both a witch and a wolf before? I thought your aunt refused because it wasn't possible—she'd lose her powers."

"Apparently, this woman wasn't bitten. This was the way she was born."

"Wait," Maria's head began to pound. "She's a witch, and she's a wolf ... and she just moved here, to Santa Cruz? Like she's here now?"

"Yes, ma'am."

Maria rolled, flopping on her back. "For fuck's sake. And you want me to take lead and deal with this?"

Tamsin gave a throaty laugh. "You know you're my favorite."

"No, I'm not. Paige is. You just need to go teach those miscreants English. Gods above, Tamsin. You owe me big. I'm too tired to figure out how or when or ... well, anything. I'll call you later and give you a piece of my mind. But I'm going back to sleep right now."

"Night, Maria. And thank you."

She barely heard her alpha's "good night" before she was back asleep.

CHAPTER 11 - DON'T TRUST ANYONE
Blake

Blake lay on the bed in the room she'd chosen. The one that used to belong to the former owner. Once she spent some time in the room, she could smell the wolf scents all around her. She watched until the clock passed five am—seven in the Midwest—then picked up the phone and dialed Mom.

She needed answers, and no matter what the coven had said the previous night, things felt weird now that her secret was out.

"Sweetie, did you make it to Cinthia's place? Why are you calling so early? Is there an emergency?"

Blake could hear her mom start to work herself into a panic. "Mom. Yes, I made it. No, no emergency. Breathe. Listen, I have questions, and I couldn't call last night."

There was a pause as she heard her mom pour herself something ... probably coffee. "What is it, sweetie?"

"Did you know there's a werewolf pack here?"

"No, I didn't. Did you run into another wolf? How did you find out they were a wolf? You smelled it on them, didn't you? Are you safe? Did the coven find out? Should you come home?"

"Stop! Mom! *Listen.* Gods above. Tell me again about this war between the witches and the wolves." Blake stared at the ceiling, wishing she could be sitting at the table with her mom, coffee in hand, keeping the woman focused.

"I've told you, sweetie. You've heard the story so many times."

"No, Mom. You told me once, as a teen, before I moved away. Humor me."

A huge sigh traveled the line. "I come from a small community in South Dakota. When I was young, our pack was strong with twenty wolves. When I was fourteen, a coven in a neighboring town decided they didn't like our pack so close and worked to run us out. My alphas resisted being pushed out."

"Did the groups talk?" Blake couldn't imagine witches just unilaterally deciding another group had to leave.

A growl, so low it gave Blake chills, came from her mom. "No. The pack received a letter telling them to relocate. It was ridiculous. We'd been in the area for generations. Then over the next six months, the wolves had a series of ... follies. Lost jobs, fatal accidents, job transfers ... you name it, it happened. The next thing we knew, there were only three wolves left, and their will to fight was gone."

"If you knew about this, how did you end up marrying Dad?" *How did I end up being born a witch-wolf freak?*

"I was one of the first of the fall-outs. I got a full scholarship to a college in Wisconsin. It was one of the better situations. I left to study in Madison and only knew about the rest when my parents died months later. Your father went to the same college and we fell in love. He agreed with keeping the secret. He knew about the animosity."

"Why didn't you ever find a pack ... you know, for you or for me?"

There was a pause. "Sweetie, you know this, we've discussed it before. To learn magic, you need a coven. Dad and I discussed it when you were young and came to a decision. I could sneak off to run at the full moon and no one was the wiser. It's hard being a lone wolf, but I had Dad ... and you, and it was okay. So, we found a coven in a town where both he and I found jobs."

"What about after he died? You left town. Did you find a new pack?" Blake didn't know why this never occurred to her before this. She'd been so caught up in her own life, but it was such an obvious question.

For a moment, Blake wondered if her mom would answer. The line was silent for too long.

"Mom? Why didn't you tell me you joined a new pack?"

"Blake, I didn't want you to follow me. You were doing so well in that coven of yours and Dad's. You had a life in Minnesota. Wolves need people, but you found a way to get that human interaction. You've never been in a pack, you don't know what you're missing. After Dad died ... I couldn't live without a pack."

"That's fine Mom, but why not tell me?"

"Because you would've sought it out yourself, and you're learning your magic. You can't have them both."

Chills ran throughout Blake's body. "One of Aunt Cinthia's coven witches can sense wolves the same way I can sense witches. She just looked at me ... and knew."

"Oh sweetie, what did you do?"

"I ran. Aunt Cinthia gave me a room here and I've locked myself in. But ... apparently the pack and the coven here are friendly."

"Blake, listen to me. Don't trust it."

She closed her eyes. "I know, Mom. I know."

A knock echoed through the room. "Blake, I heard you talking. Would you like tea or coffee?" Aunt Cinthia still sounded welcoming. "I could make you some breakfast. I was thinking a breakfast sandwich, if you're interested."

"Yeah, Cinthia, give me a few minutes to get dressed. Sounds great." Blake lowered her voice. "Mom, Cinthia's up. I'm gonna go, get some coffee, check in with her. I'll update you later."

"Don't forget, sweetie, you can always come here. Maybe you've learned enough magic; maybe it's time to embrace the wolf. You haven't unpacked the truck, have you?"

"Love you too, Mom." Blake ended the call and checked the time. Past six, time to face the ... witch.

She slipped on a clean pair of jeans and t-shirt. In the bathroom she splashed water on her face. *Okay, Blake. You can do this. If nothing else, you saw California, experienced the West Coast, and now you can head back to the Midwest.* Making a face at herself in the mirror, she turned to face her future.

CHAPTER 12 - THAT ISN'T HOW IT WORKS
Maria

Waking up for the second time, Maria squeezed her eyes shut and pulled the covers over her head. She still didn't want to face the day. The heavenly scent of coffee wafted up to her room. She peeked out from her covers and saw it was only six o'clock. *Still before eight? Why am I up this early? It's only been an extra hour.* With the sunlight cutting across her room, Maria knew she wasn't getting any more sleep. She gave up, threw back the covers, and rolled out of bed.

By her closet, she pulled on a clean lavender spring dress with matching belt and trudged to the kitchen. On the way down the stairs, she finger-combed her hair into a semblance of the same direction and secured the unruly locks into a high ponytail.

She found Orin sitting with bagels and donuts in the kitchen. She let out a groan, pouring a mug of his glorious brew and flopping next to him. He slid over a plate with a pastry covered in pink frosting and sprinkles. She moaned, tasting her first bite, washing it down with his divine ambrosia.

"To what do I owe this treat? Why are you up this early? And making coffee?"

Orin smiled. "Connie mumbled something before collapsing a few hours ago. It was probably full sentences, but I was still asleep. I checked my phone at five thirty and she'd left a text. I decided the house needed a nice wake-up today, it being a full moon."

Maria reached over and hugged him. She then explained her morning call with Tamsin. "I'm calling in sick. I'm going to text Cinthia and see when I can go and meet this wonder woman: half witch, half wolf, all mystery."

"I love the idea of growing the pack, Maria, but we can't have a witch living under this roof. If Clyde couldn't move his mate here ..."

"Orin, I haven't met the woman yet, but from what I understand, she's a wolf."

"And a witch."

"I dunno; it's all above my paygrade. I just need to play host. I've never even heard of such a thing."

"Me, either, and there's a reason for it. We may get along with the witches here, and in most cities ... now, but historically that wasn't the case."

"I don't need a history lesson; I've had plenty." Maria drank more coffee. "Your coffee is good, but not good enough for a lecture."

He laughed. "Fine. I guess this is really something we need to discuss with Tamsin."

"Yeah, you do that. Tell Tamsin what to do with the pack. Have fun with that."

Orin rubbed his face. "Fair enough."

Finishing her donut, Maria took out her phone. Hi, Cinthia, it's me, Maria. I was asked to play ambassador for the pack. Let me know a good time for you and the new coven member.

Maria expected the response to take some time, so she went to fill her coffee. She decided she'd send a note to work next. When she opened her phone, Cinthia had already replied.

Maria! Excellent! I couldn't have selected a better representative. Blake and I were just talking about how the coven and pack get along here in Santa Cruz. You're welcome at any point. Come on over, my friend.

I wonder if Blake comes from an old-school coven where the wolves and witches don't get along.

Maria shot off an email to her boss explaining why she wasn't coming in for the day, then finished her mug of coffee. She cleaned up her mess and selected a second donut for the road. Opening up the text messages, she sent to Cinthia, `On my way, see you soon.`

She debated walking—the day was beautiful—but decided to drive. Who knew where this day would end up. It didn't take her long. She parked behind a huge moving van and skipped up the stairs of the house that used to be Clyde and Elinor's home. She never did understand the werewolf decree that stated witches couldn't live in a pack house.

As much as she loved the house, there would've been no harm in Elinor and Clyde living in the alpha suite in the back of the pack house. *The rule seems so antiquated to me, born of a time when people didn't understand that we are all just people.*

She knocked, and Cinthia answered, pulling her into a hug. "Maria, don't you look lovely this morning!" With long, black, wavy hair and brown eyes, the older coven leader always looked perfect. She wore a patchwork dress and a dark purple shawl.

The scent of coffee wafted out. "As do you, Cinthia."

"Come in, come in. I have coffee and tea, and I've made breakfast sandwiches. Only one of my guests is up right now, but it's the one you want to speak with, so it's all good."

Maria followed Cinthia in, and paused when she saw the other woman. Blake—it had to be Blake, it was who she was here to meet—had stunning blue eyes, the color of the ocean on a stormy day. Her blond hair flowed in slight waves past her shoulders. As Maria entered she stood, and though she wore jeans and a t-shirt, Maria could tell she was fit in the smooth, liquid way she moved.

Mouth dry, she tried to swallow. She was here to represent the wolves, not drool over a Midwest beauty. *Get yourself together, woman!* Mechanically, she held out her hand. "Hi! I'm, um, Maria. I'm from, um, the local pack. I'd like to, ah, welcome you."

One of her beautifully sculpted eyebrows rose as she crossed the room and took Maria's hand. Blake's hand was smooth and her handshake was solid, nothing limp or annoying. "Nice to meet you, Maria. I'm Blake. You didn't have to go out of your way to come over here. I don't even know if I'm staying in the area."

Maria tightened her hand as if she could keep the other woman here by sheer force of will alone. "Oh? Why not?"

The other woman's eyes widened a bit. "I, ah, I'm not sure. I've never met any other wolves, um, werewolves, besides my mom."

Smiling wide, Maria leaned in closer. "So, I'm your first?"

Blake laughed. "I didn't think I had many firsts left, but yes, that's what I'm saying."

"Well, good. Maybe we can find other 'firsts' around here for you to enjoy." *What the hell am I doing? Am I flirting with a woman I just met? And this early in the morning? What am I thinking? I should've gotten more sleep ... that's it.*

With a small shake of her head to clear it, Maria forced herself to release Blake's hand.

"Coffee, Maria?" Cinthia asked from the kitchen. "I know I'm not up to Orin's level—Clyde and Elinore talked about his coffee all the time—but I think I can at least make it palatable."

Maria's shoulders loosened and she walked to the kitchen island hoping the caffeine would be a lifeline. "That would be amazing. And you mentioned a breakfast sandwich? I've only had donuts today. The sugar may be addling my synapses. Something with real food parts sounds great."

Blake took the stool next to hers and their legs touched. A shiver shot through Maria, but she closed her eyes and decided to ignore it. She was here to meet Blake, maybe introduce her to the pack. Whatever that shiver was, it had no place in today's agenda.

"Blake," Maria began. "Tell me about how you've gotten to be ... twenty ..."

"Thirty."

"Mmm. Thirty. Okay, good age." *Stop thinking about dating her. She'll probably be back in the Midwest in a day or two. Dating! Coffee, drink more coffee.* "Thirty, and you've never met another wolf."

As they ate, Maria slowly coaxed Blake's story from her. By the end, she was amazed the woman had been running as a wolf for over twenty-two years, and had never done it with anyone but her mom. "Would you like to run with our pack tonight?"

Blake jerked back as if hit. "What? No. I couldn't. I'll just, you know." Her hand flew up around her head. "Do ... something."

Maria clasped the other woman's hand. For a moment, she reveled in its texture. "There isn't a 'something' to do. Run with our pack. It'll be safer, especially since you're new to the area, and it's fun ... trust me." She gave Blake's hand a squeeze.

Blake bit her lip, and heat boiled in Maria's gut. *What is going on?* The other woman finally shrugged. "Okay, fine, yeah. I'll run with all of you. Maybe doing it once will get it out of my system."

Oh, honey, that isn't how it works. You are just the cutest.

Clomping on the stairs had them all turning to look. Another woman, with short brown hair, came around the corner. She looked ready to spit someone and spin them over a fire. She focused on Maria and glared as if spying a good candidate. "Are you witch or wolf?"

Wanting to laugh, Maria finally released Blake's hand and gave the other woman her full attention. "Why, lovely lady, you must be Gretel."

The woman's eyes narrowed. "You heard me. Witch or wolf?"

Cinthia came from around the counter, fists on her hips. "I don't know what it's like in Minnesota, but you do not speak to other people like that around here. You have a few options, but if you don't learn manners and respect, living in Santa Cruz will *not* be one of them."

Gretel blanched. "You'd choose a wolf over a coven member?"

"I would, if the coven member was acting like you are now. I have expectations for respect in my witches, young lady. I know you have a lot of new things in your life right now, but manners are always expected."

Face hard, Gretel spun on her heel and stomped away.

CHAPTER 13 - DOESN'T MEAN EVERYONE IS GAY!
Blake

Blake heard the door close with finality. It felt like a dagger in her heart. She remembered ten years earlier when Gretel's family had brought the gangly eleven-year-old to a coven meeting. She was just coming into her abilities, and in Blake's eyes, she glowed a light reddish brown, a combination of fire and earth. She was better with the fire, but she had proficiencies in both.

At the time, Blake was twenty, and Gretel looked up to her. Blake and Chey became two of her teachers, leading her through the basics. Blake's specialty was plant magic, green magic. She could grow anything, anywhere. She also had an affinity for animals, a streak of yellow magic, but not many people saw it.

Though she didn't share any proficiencies with Gretel and couldn't guide her, she could help with the basics of what it meant to be a witch. She'd never taught the girl to hate wolves. From what she'd witnessed, neither had Chey. *Fuck! I wonder if she's calling Chey right now to bitch about me, or if she did last night. Maybe I've lost my other best friend, too. Why am I too scared to call her and find out?*

Blake shook her head and turned back to Cinthia and Maria. Gah! Maria, the spitfire werewolf who wanted to spend some time with her today. The woman was tiny and voluptuous, just her type. Blake was pretty sure the other woman had flirted with her, but wasn't positive. *Just because I'm in California, doesn't mean everyone is gay!* She let her eyes travel over the other woman's curves. *But it would be nice.*

She rubbed her temples. *What am I thinking? I haven't been this out of control since I was a teen!*

"So, Maria," Cinthia said, placing a plate with a breakfast sandwich in front of her. "Now that the evil alpha of the west is gone, have you started dating?"

She even blushes divinely!

Maria took a bite and moaned. Blake almost bolted from the room. "Why is everyone worried about my social life?"

Cinthia laughed. "Gossip, dear; everyone loves gossip."

"Georgette signed me up for one of those dating apps. The first date—" She made a face.

"It didn't go well?"

"Gods above, he wanted me to be a stay-at-home wife. He thought I didn't know what 'IT' meant when I'd put it down for my occupation."

Blake winced when Maria said 'he.' So much for their earlier flirting. She gazed more openly at her, with her big brown eyes, and full mouth. There were things she'd like to do with this wolf. *I wonder if other wolves have more stamina, too?* She picked up the coffee Cinthia refilled to take a hesitant sip.

"Well, dear, what did you learn from that date?"

"Probably that men aren't worth it."

Cinthia smiled. "Any other dates on the horizon?"

The other woman slumped as if not happy with the situation. "Maybe. I've found a few women that look promising."

Blake perked up, almost scalding her tongue in the process. Putting the mug on the counter, she swallowed to make sure everything in her mouth still worked. "You, ah, like men *and* women?"

Maria smiled at her. "I do. I usually stick to women though. I hope that doesn't scare you off. You know things are ... I dunno how it is where you're from, but around here it isn't a big deal. Just like how we aren't as uptight between witches and wolves." Maria waggled her eyebrows at Blake. "Maybe more firsts for you?"

"You'd be surprised. Not everything will be a first."

Maria's smile widened. "Fair enough." She sipped her coffee. "So, tonight. Do you want to come to the pack house, have dinner, meet the other wolves, then come run with us?"

Blake leaned away. "I'm really more comfortable running alone."

"No." Maria shook her head. "It isn't really an option. You don't know anything about packs, wolves, lone wolves, and the rules, do you?"

Cinthia tilted her head. "Why don't you two take a walk, tour the area, and you can explain the ways of wolves before throwing her *to* the wolves. And don't think I didn't notice you changing the subject. I'm so curious about that second date."

Maria groaned. "Nope, awful. I hate dating, it's official. The next one is Friday, and I'm already regretting it."

Cinthia laughed as Maria headed to the door. Halfway there, Maria looked over her shoulder. "Well? Are you coming?"

The image created had Blake biting back her first response as her body tightened. She wondered if Maria did anything casual.

Outside, she glared at the moving van. Maria laughed, the sound filling Blake. Nothing small about her emotions. "You didn't enjoy driving half way across the country to get here?"

"No, and if I decide this joint community is too much, I have to turn around and head back." Blake shivered. "That sounds like all sorts of hell."

Maria hooked her arm in Blake's, and her body tingled at the sensation. *Gods above, the other woman had better be feeling some of this as well.*

They walked a few blocks in silence, Maria letting her take in the sights. It didn't take long for them to get to an area with fewer homes and more shops. "So, my new friend, do you need anything?"

Yes! So many things. "Ah, no. I think I brought everything I need from home ... well, Minnesota."

"What did you do there, you know, for work?"

"I danced."

"Like in a troupe?"

"Like on a pole."

Maria stopped, eyes wide, then her mouth dropped open. Facing Blake she slowly looked her up and down from head to toe.

Blake's confidence grew the more the other woman gaped. "Like what you see?"

Maria blanched. "Sorry, I, ah ... I mean, okay, I'm sure you can get something like that if that's what you're interested in." She started to pull away, but Blake held onto her arm, liking that they walked linked together.

With a steadying breath, Maria relaxed, then giggled. "That must be fun, and freeing. I bet that's how you survived living without a pack. Wolves need people, and contact. You probably got plenty of contact there."

It was Blake's turn to laugh. This woman was a surprise at every turn. "So, you're not disgusted?"

There was a moment where they went back to walking in silence, then Maria huffed out a laugh. "Disgusted? No. Intrigued. I think I'm hoping you get that job just so I can go and watch."

Blake jerked her head down in time to see the other woman blush and duck away. "Have you ever been to a strip club?"

"No. I always thought it was scantily-clad women and horny men. Not really my scene."

"You don't want to see the women?"

"The men."

Blake smiled as the two continued to walk and tour Santa Cruz. These wolves just may not be so bad after all.

CHAPTER 14 - IS YOUR ROOM ON THE TOUR?
Maria

"Stop pacing. Either she comes, or she doesn't. What's your problem?" Georgette put down her book and gazed at Maria with a blank stare.

"Nothing's my problem. This girl, she's never run with a pack. I was the first wolf besides her mom she's ever met. She needs us, but doesn't realize it. What if she doesn't come?" The thought made Maria's gut clench. She couldn't believe how much it meant to her to have Blake join them, but in all likelihood, she wouldn't.

Georgette grumbled. "She's what? Thirty? She'll be fine. It isn't like she'll run into us if she doesn't want to. Now, sit, relax, and wait on Connie and Orin finishing dinner. We get Connie's cooking one night a month; relax and enjoy."

Maria spun on her heel and collapsed on one of the couches. She let her arm fall over her eyes and she breathed in deeply. Connie worked at a high-end American style restaurant. When she cooked for the pack, she made the kind of food she grew up cooking, things she'd never be able to cook at the restaurant. Homestyle meals that stuck to your ribs. But as a four Michelin star chef, the food was always fantastic. Georgette was right that looking forward to their monthly meal was worth it.

She needed to stop and relax. Slow breath in ... slow breath out. As her body sank into the couch, Maria smelled the deep aromas of

Italian spices. Her stomach growled. "Connie, what are you making, and how long will it take?"

A laugh floated from the kitchen. "The lasagna will be done in about five minutes. Will this new wolf be here by then?"

Maria heard Orin say something in response to that, and Connie snapped back. She wasn't sure if she wanted to know what they were fighting about.

The front door opened and Maria sat up and watched to see who came in. Next to her, Georgette snorted. "It has to be Tory, idiot. Everyone else is here. The new wolf would knock."

Maria slumped, realizing Georgette was right. *Damn it, what's wrong with me? It's not like this is a date or anything. Blake is a new wolf who can come run with us or not. I need to calm myself down and prepare for the run.*

About to turn around, she heard laughing and talking coming from the front door. "And this is the main room. It's big and comfortable. As you can see, it fits more than the five of us currently living here."

Maria stood so quickly her head spun. She twisted and almost ended up on her ass. Tory came in leading the tall, blond knockout. Maria's heart beat faster as Blake gazed around the room.

"I can give you a full tour?" Tory asked, standing next to her. "Do you want to see the rest of the place?"

Maria stepped forward. "I can do it, Tory. You just got home from work. Do you want to go change, or rest for a moment before dinner?"

Tory shook her head to say 'no,' but Georgette answered first. "Tory, come tell me about your day. Any big exciting stories from the hospital?"

Shrugging, Tory sat next to Georgette. Maria headed over to Blake. "So, want a tour before dinner?"

The smile Blake gave her sent tingles all the way down to her toes. *This isn't normal. I probably should've let Tory give the tour ... but I'm enjoying Blake's company too much.* "Sure, yeah. Sounds great."

They walked through the living room to the dining room kitchen area. "This is Connie, she's an amazing chef. She works downtown at Ocean Sunrise, a swank restaurant. She only cooks for us once a month, so this was the perfect day to meet her. Orin there is her husband, he works from home in the marketing biz."

Blake smiled at them.

Connie gave her a wide smile. "Welcome to the madhouse, Blake. I hear this is your first time around a pack of wolves."

Blake huffed. "Yeah. You all are very gregarious. I'm used to the witches, they tend to be a bit less ..." Her sentence trailed off as she seemed to realize she didn't know how to end without sounding rude.

The wolves are just so much larger than life in so many ways. She'll have to get used to it.

Orin rolled his eyes. "Well, if you're more used to the witches ..."

Connie hit her husband upside the head. "Ignore him. He's spent too much time with the wrong wolves. We love that you're here, friend."

Maria glared at Orin. She hooked her arm in Blake's, trying to ignore the shiver that ran throughout her body ... again. "Through this door is our backyard. It's private, and new wolves can play."

They headed out and she pointed out the unique areas of the lot. There was a fire pit, an area for a barbeque, and the fence in the back where they exited when they wolfed out. The two of them re-entered the pack house through a different set of sliding doors. "Down this hallway we have a game room with a pool table, darts, and a small bar—not that alcohol does much for us. This door leads to the basement. There is a theater room and an area for kids to play."

"How many kids in your pack?"

Maria sighed. "There used to be more, but right now there aren't any."

Blake pointed to the stairs. "What's up there?"

"Bedrooms. There are some down here as well."

"Is your room up there?"

Maria's stomach clenched. She licked her lips, though her mouth was dry. "Yeah, it is."

Blake leaned down, touching her lips to Maria's ear. "Is that on the tour?"

Tightening her hold on Blake's arm, she opened up her mouth to answer, when

Connie's voice rang out. "Dinner, come and get it."

With a nervous chuckle, Maria pulled Blake back to the dining room. The table was loaded with lasagna, garlic bread, salad, and brussel sprouts. Everything looked and smelled delicious. Loading up plates, they all dug in. Next to her, Blake groaned. "Do you always eat like this? Because a person could get used to this ... this is fantastic."

Connie blushed and Georgette laughed. "Oh, no, new girl. We can only convince Connie to cook rarely. But if you go to her restaurant, Ocean Sunrise, you get the family discount, and it's just as good there."

Tory leaned back. "So, Blake, what do you do ... or will you do once you find a job?"

Blake smiled and winked at the younger woman, then stared directly at Orin daring him to comment. "I'm an exotic dancer." Her gazed moved to Connie. "One day, I'd love to start a nursery. Growing plants has always been one of my big loves and I'm good. I can grow anything anywhere. I've been dancing, it earns enough to save money. I figure I'll have the money soon ... though with the move, who knows."

Orin had rolled his eyes at the small jab, but smiled good-naturedly. The longer the meal went on, the less cantankerous he was. Maria wasn't sure why he'd been such a sourpuss.

After they ate a few more bites, Blake bit her lip. "So, where do you run? This building is in such a great spot, it feels like a tourist trap."

Georgette looked out the back. "If you notice, the backyard butts up to a small stretch of undeveloped land. It isn't a lot, but it's preserved for hiking. We can slip out the back and run through there and it leads to a larger forested area a few miles inland. It's great to not have to drive anywhere to run."

Blake gazed at everyone. "So, what, we all go out, strip naked in front of each other, and go? No wonder nobody blinked at my occupation."

The laughter warmed Maria. Blake would fit in just fine.

CHAPTER 15 - IF IT MEANS I GET TO SEE YOU STRIP
Blake

Walking into the pack house with the tiny Tory, Blake felt every muscle in her body tense. But once she met the pack, she finally understood why her mom had left after Dad had died. This was what had been missing all those years. There were small touches and nonverbal communication throughout dinner.

On one side of her sat Maria, and those touches made her heart hiccup. But Connie had sat on the other side, and the older woman had touched her arm and shoulder, her leg, and even brushed her cheek. Every small swipe of her fingers made Blake relax a pinch more. She never realized how much she craved human ... wolf? ... interaction.

Maria leaned over. "Are you ready to get your fur on?"

Blake whispered soft enough she hoped no one else would hear. "If it means I get to see you strip, then definitely."

The rosy color that took over Maria's neck and face was worth it.

Tory and Georgette started clearing the dishes. Blake watched them for a moment. "Do you two want help?"

Georgette snorted. "Go, get out there and start the change, we'll be out in a minute. Wait for us in the backyard. Connie and Orin want a minute to drink a coffee while we clean. That will give Blake a bit of privacy instead of having to deal with all of us." Georgette turned to

Blake. "Unless you'd rather Tory or someone else. We figure one wolf this time."

Blake gazed at the three other women. "I do work at a strip club back home, but thanks. Sure, I'll take Maria." She tried to sound blasé, but wasn't sure if she pulled it off.

Maria slid her arm into Blake's, a move that was becoming familiar in a single day, and led her back outside. "Okay, we usually fold, or toss, our clothes in the chairs over here and shift. Since you're new—to the pack, to California, to running with others—we want you to have some time to get used to everything. It's going to overwhelm you. Not as much as a new wolf, but close."

"I haven't been a new wolf since I was eight."

Maria slid her arm all the way around Blake's back. "I know, or rather, I could've guessed, but this place will smell different. *I'll* smell different. It'll be ... new."

Blake stopped moving. She stopped breathing. She hadn't considered how everything would smell, how Maria the wolf would smell. She turned to gaze into the dark brown eyes of the smaller woman. "Okay, you're right. This is going to be freaky. How about a kiss for good luck?"

The eyes staring at her widened, and Blake thought Maria would back up. But then slowly, very slowly she nodded. Blake's hand shook as she used a finger to tip Maria's chin up. She lowered her head and lightly brushed her lips across the other woman's.

Fireworks went off in her head and she breathed in sharply through her nose before pulling away. Maria's mouth hung slightly open. Her tongue darted out to wet her lips as she gazed up at Blake. "Okay, right, let's strip and shift."

As if it took work, the smaller woman yanked her body to the side and moved over to the lawn chairs. In one swift motion she pulled off her dress. Blake let out a small squeak when she realized the other woman hadn't worn anything under the dress. It made sense if all they'd planned on doing was coming out to run. Her backside was perfect.

Maria looked at Blake over her shoulder. "Are you joining me?"

Broken from her trance, Blake made her way to the chairs. "Yeah ... yes ... of course." *Anytime you want, Ms. Perfect-naked.*

It took her a few extra minutes to strip down, and fold her clothes. Once she did, Maria was a gray wolf with black markings. She got down on her hands and knees and shut her eyes. It didn't take long for the change to come over her, and then everything was different.

The scents that overtook her weren't the oak trees and pine she was used to, but Eucalyptus and grasses she didn't recognize. She started sniffing around the backyard, cataloging everything. When something interested her, she dug her nose in deeper, inhaling every nuance. When she backed up, she always saw Maria, who stayed near her, bobbing her head as if keeping track of what she focused on.

It was ... almost too much, but it was fantastic. Once she'd circled the backyard, the wind brought the scent of Maria to her. She smelled ... divine. She wasn't sure what it was, but it made her feel drunk. An overwhelming need brought her closer to the other woman. She needed more of that smell in her nose. Looking around at the flowers, fence, and house, Blake realized she'd missed the other four wolves coming out to shift.

The first wolf she came up to was small and tawny in color like Blake. Unlike Blake, who had no other markings, this wolf had black paws. Taking in Connie's scent, it wasn't as tantalizing as Maria, but it smelled ... friendly.

The next wolf, a gray wolf like Maria, but with a white tail and white markings, smelled ... amused. Georgette. She trotted away once Blake got a good sniff.

The next one stood by Connie, a red and black wolf. Being the only male wolf, Orin was simple to pick out of the crowd.

Tory was a small black wolf, and she was hopping around, ready to go.

As a pack, they headed out a small door in the back fence. Blake stayed in the middle of the group; she'd never seen this many wolves. They moved like the wind, and despite their number, they barely made a sound. Soon after their run started, Blake could feel the area open up.

The scents around her changed. A deer had run through, but the odor was old. A couple of dogs crossed this trail regularly, following the paths of the feral cats that lived in the den of the dead tree. Above her, she heard the familiar chitter of squirrels and the occasional skittering of lizards through the branches of the trees.

Blake wanted to stretch her legs and go. The others apparently wanted to move as well, because as a group they spent some time just running. Eventually, Connie howled to the moon, and the others followed suit. Birds scattered to the sky at the sudden sound, a cacophony of beating wings, and Blake felt free and alive. She couldn't believe it could be like this.

They found a trail that led to a lone cougar, and they were off. She watched as the pack worked as a group to bring the beast down.

At a small lake, they drank their fill. Then they took off running again. The wind ruffled her fur and the trees reached out to scratch her. She felt alive. Her body exuded her pleasure with the world around her and it felt like beams of sunshine radiated from her fur.

A snarl stopped her in her tracks. Turning quickly, Blake stared into Orin's disapproving brown eyes and snarling muzzle. Then, gaping, she saw a wild jungle of plants growing behind them. Her magic had escaped her. All the plants she'd run across had fed on her magic and flourished. They'd become more.

Tail tucked, she lowered her head under the disappointment of the others. They didn't want her. They thought she was a freak. She turned tail and ran.

CHAPTER 16 - VIBRATIONS CAN BE EXCITING
Tamsin

It should be illegal for full moons to happen midweek! Tamsin tried to stop the obnoxious noises coming from her phone before they woke Paige up, too, but her body felt sluggish and heavy. They'd run later than she'd planned, chasing down some rabbits.

It being her partner's second run ever, she was thrilled how much pleasure she took at their late-night shenanigans, but now, knowing it was a school day, Tamsin debated her wisdom. Then again, Paige's obvious delight made the run worth it.

Tamsin rolled from bed, barely balancing on her feet. It was getting to be late May; why was it still so damn cold? *I need slippers, soft fuzzy bunny slippers to warm my feet on these damn cold floors. Even in Santa Cruz, if I remember correctly, the floors are cold!*

Padding to the bathroom, she debated turning on the water, but decided she needed coffee first. She trudged to the kitchen to turn on the kettle for the French press and filled the container with a seductive smelling ground coffee bean, a present from another teacher at the school where she taught. Sadness gripped her gut. *It's going to be really hard to leave my friends there.*

Sighing, she sniffed the coffee beans, imagining the party where a bunch of teachers swapped gifts. She'd given a math teacher a shirt that said, 'I Rule' over a ruler. She sniffed again, almost swooned at how good the ground bean smelled. *Now that will warm me up better than silly bunny slippers.*

She knew the kettle wouldn't take long—maybe a minute or two—so she pulled out a bagel, butter, bread, peanut butter, and jelly. Water ready, she poured it over the grounds, and left the food for after her shower. She then went to take a quick shower. The coffee would need about five minutes, and she didn't plan to take much more than that to wash off the run.

Wrapped in a warm robe, she pressed the coffee grounds down then went to dress. Jeans and a long sleeve t-shirt with a wolf howling at the moon. The black and white shirt fit her mood for the day.

Back in the kitchen, she made the PB&J for lunch, the bagel for breakfast. A few more items went in her lunch bag. She poured the coffee into a travel mug, a quick kiss for Paige, who grumbled groggily in her sleep, and she was ready to face high schoolers ... if anyone was ever ready for that.

Tamsin loved teaching English. She'd been applying for jobs in and around Santa Cruz. If she didn't get a job teaching, she knew the pack had money and she had time ... she just wanted to do more with her life than be the pack's alpha. The challenge of relating to teenagers invigorated her and kept her on her toes. She really hoped she found an environment she enjoyed teaching in as much as she loved her current one.

As she taught throughout the morning and students moved in and out of her classes, her phone kept buzzing. Thankfully, being in her pocket, none of the students heard it.

She couldn't remember such an active morning in months. Just before fourth period, she saw that every member of the pack—and Cinthia—had texted her. She quickly read through the messages.

Connie, at three in the morning. *It must have been right after their run.* Blake, the new wolf is great, but there's an issue. We need to talk.

Damn, maybe I should've checked these this morning before work ... but no, I didn't have the bandwidth for that after the long night last night.

Orin, at eight. *Early riser.* I don't like the idea of a witch in our pack, T. I know she's a wolf, but you'll need to make a decision.

He is acting weird. He's always been the backbone of the pack! What is up with him?

Cinthia, quarter after eight. Morning, Tam. Blake came home and locked herself in your old room. I feel her fear and desperation. I don't know what happened, she was hopeful when she left. I hope you can help her … or Maria. There's a real connection there.

A connection? Interesting …

Tory, eight thirty. Working all day. Thanks for letting me join. First run last night. Great to be home.

Tamsin laughed at the lightness in Tory's message. Apparently whatever happened flitted right over the young wolf's head.

Maria, eight thirty. Tam, we need to talk. Blake needs us.

There was a few minutes between the texts as if Maria needed to think.

I think Orin scared her off last night. He has something against witches. I'm not sure what. I need your help.

After a few minutes there was another text from her. Tamsin could almost see Maria agonizing over her words.

We need your help.

I need to get to the bottom of Orin's animosity. I need to get home to the pack. A warmth infused her as she realized she was truly back to thinking of Santa Cruz and the pack house as home. It'd been years since her center had been California, but in a few weeks, and thanks to Paige, she'd completely refocused.

Georgette, nine thirty. Morning! Don't know if you heard. Blake ran with us last night. Her magic escaped her. It was a trip. Want a picture? I could go take one.

On a separate note, I think.

There was a break. Tamsin could see Georgette pacing as she typed, erased and retyped, coming up with the exact thing she wanted to say.

I don't know, I want to talk to you about Blake and Maria. But not over text.

Not exactly what I expected, but if anyone knows Maria, it's Georgette. The two of them are like sisters. Cinthia may be right about the connection.

Maria, quarter to ten. At work. I've had time to think about this. I probably don't need your help with that issue. Blake does, though. Sorry if I freaked you out. I'm good.

Paige, ten. Hi, love, thanks for letting me sleep in this morning. Last night was amazing. The run, the hunt, all of it.

Nolan, quarter past ten. Just confirming our appointment for tonight at the gym?

Tamsin sighed. The last two were the easiest. She told Paige she loved her, too. Then, she shot off a confirmation to Nolan.

She had a free period for forty minutes from eleven thirty-five to twelve fifteen. Students usually hung out in her room, but she could shut the door. She sent off texts to all her pack asking if they could join in a group call at eleven-thirty ... er, nine-thirty their time.

The next class slipped by quickly, and when Tamsin initiated the virtual meeting, only Orin, Maria, and Connie were there.

"Georgette's in a meeting. She said she'll talk with you later." Maria shrugged as if it weren't a big deal. They'd all texted as soon as they woke up, this couldn't be 'nothing.'

Connie's eyes roved the faces on the screen. "I don't know why Tory couldn't make it. Couldn't she get a fifteen minute break?"

Tamsin shook her head. "She was called into a patient's room. Her text this morning was the only one that didn't involve Blake, so I'm confident you all can catch the others up."

Orin snorted. "You mean the freaking witch."

Connie snarked, "Do you want to sleep alone tonight?"

"Can someone please tell me what happened?" Tamsin's voice snapped out in a low snarl, shutting them all up. *Why can't they welcome someone to the pack without me? They've been without an alpha ... a real alpha for so long, since Clyde died. They're better than this.* For a moment, Tamsin fought uncharacteristic self doubt. Was this because she was a weak leader, or because of what Vernon had done? Or was it the pack itself?

Connie filled her in. Tamsin wished she'd seen the plants grow; it would've been amazing, like a movie come to life. "So, you were in a forest, an area we know no one ever goes but us ... what's the issue?"

Orin gaped. "What's the issue? She's a witch! The laws are clear."

"Are they laws?"

"Of course they're laws."

Tamsin sighed. "Okay, find the specific laws and their wording. We need to know exactly what we're dealing with. I need to know if this is something every wolf pack knows. I'll talk with the other alphas."

Maria's face scrunched up. "So, what's my role? Do I continue to help her out? Am I still her link to the pack?"

Tamsin slowly bobbed her head up and down. "Yes, but let her reach out to you."

After that, the call turned to more general news about the pack. Tamsin ended the call with about twenty minutes to get work done.

At the end of the day, she made her way to the gym. As always, Nolan beat her there. He'd decided on the elliptical for his warm-up.

They worked out for about five minutes before Nolan gave Tamsin a wide smile. "Have fun last night?"

Tamsin smiled warmly back. "We did. It was only Paige's second run ... well, full moon run, and she frolicked."

"How is your group back home doing?"

A low guttural growl escaped her.

Nolan laughed. "Something happen?"

"Can I ask you a question?"

"Sure, but I may not know the answer."

"What do you know about the law separating witches and wolves?"

Nolan rubbed his chin. "Not a lot. You'll have to call that question in. But it isn't what you think. Can I tell you a story?"

"Please." Tamsin needed the distraction and had a feeling Nolan knew much more than she did on this topic.

"This happened years ago, like, thirty or forty years ago, over in South Dakota."

Tamsin reached over and adjusted the resistance on Nolan's and then her elliptical.

Nolan grimaced before continuing. "There was a pack, twenty strong, or so, that was almost taken out by a group of black witches."

"Wait, but there's a pack there now, some of my old pack lives there. I'm hoping they'll return to Santa Cruz once we stabilize."

"Are you listening to a story, or are we having a discussion?"

Tamsin rolled her eyes, and waved her hand for Nolan to speak.

His smile returned. "So, the witches sent a letter telling the wolves to leave. When they didn't, they threw a dispersal curse on the pack. For some, the wolves just left ... especially the younger ones. They headed off to college, job transferred, you know, opportunities they couldn't refuse. For some, there were fatal accidents: rock climbs gone wrong, sudden black ice on the road, a robbery gone bad. The alphas called in help, but by the time it came, there were only three left to save."

"Gods above. Seventeen dead or gone?" Tamsin shivered.

"Two of the alphas had invited the covens from the neighboring towns to come and help. It ended up being two covens ... well, not full covens, they had five witches each—I guess that's enough—and a dozen wolves. The group destroyed the black witches."

"How strong are black witches?"

"Individually? Strong. Stronger than a wolf, stronger than a single good witch. But a coven, working together ... I guess it doesn't get much more powerful than that."

CHAPTER 17 - JOIN THE CIRCUS
Blake

Blake paced the living room, glad she was alone. She'd never fit in, but before, she'd always been the only one who knew it. She'd been a fool to think she could waltz in and a pack would just welcome her. She knew she wasn't one of them. *I'm too much of a witch for the wolves ... and for the witches, I'm just a wolf.*

She didn't belong anywhere.

I could pack up and head to Mom, she's part of a pack ... but what if they kick me out, too? Restless, she headed to the kitchen and put the kettle on for tea. "Tea or coffee?" she mumbled to herself while she searched the cupboards.

Will they kick me out? I would ruin Mom's life as well as my own if I move in with her. I can't do that to her. Blake found a mug and decided to make tea. She poured the hot water in the mug then fidgeted with her hands as the tea steeped.

At least Aunt Cinthia doesn't reject who I am. No, I can't take the chance that Mom's pack would discover I'm a witch and have it backfire on her.

Having made a decision to not ruin her mom's life, Blake took the tea to the living room and sank into the couch and fingered a notebook. *I need to decide what to do if I'm going to stay here. Find a job, find an apartment, figure out if starting a nursery will ever be in my future ... or run off and join a circus.*

She snorted. Adding "joining the circus" to any list was her way of whistling in the dark. She'd always felt kind of like a freak, but now others around her knew it for a fact.

The door to the house opened and she tensed. Familiar voices floated in from the entryway.

"Don't worry, Gretel, I think you're a great addition to the coven. I know you're not comfortable around the wolves, but in all honesty, there isn't *that* much interaction between us and them."

Blake rolled her head and saw Gretel entering the kitchen with Sage, one of the other coven members. She couldn't figure Sage out. The woman had sandy blond hair, hazel eyes, and always wore peasant-style blouses. She was about Gretel's height. Based on her reddish aura, she could do fire magic, but the color was off, somehow. Hazy. Blake didn't have the energy to work out why. No one else could see magical auras, so there wasn't a manual. Maybe she was just tired. There was too much going on since she arrived, and perhaps Sage stealing her best friend was clouding her judgment.

Gretel headed to the refrigerator while Sage opened the pantry. "So, I can stay part of the coven and not worry about interacting with wolves too often ... that is, except for Blake."

Sage dropped a loaf of bread on the counter and turned to the upper cupboards. "Honestly, yeah. I rarely interact with any of the werewolves, but there aren't that many in town right now. Even our coven was waning until you two came. Both groups were struggling. Who knows?"

Gretel dumped a bunch of stuff on the counter, her lower lip caught in her teeth. "I mean, I've been friends with Blake for years, and it's never been an issue. I don't know if the wolf comes from her mom, or dad, or if she was bitten, but everyone in her family was so nice. Maybe I'm wrong."

"I don't know. You'll have to figure that out yourself, Gretel. I tend to avoid them myself. A bitten witch can't do magic. I don't want to take any chances." Sage began making their lunch.

Gretel's jaw dropped. "Then how can Blake be a wolf *and* do magic?"

Sage laughed. "She couldn't have been bitten, of course. She was born as both. I don't know that I've ever heard of such a thing. But, then again, who am I to know anything? Just know, if you get bitten, then you're all wolf."

"Why would I get bitten?"

There was a moment of silence before Sage spoke. "I mean, you probably won't, but who knows. A wolf *could* lose control, right?"

Blake clenched her jaw. Breathing slowly in and out through her nose, she tried to relax her fingers from digging into the couch pillows. She'd been friends with Gretel for ten years and had never accidentally bitten any witch; why would it suddenly happen now? But people who were scared made strange logical leaps.

Finally, the two packed their meals in bags, put their dishes in the sink, and headed out. Not once did they look into the living room or notice they weren't alone. *If Gretel and I ever become friends again, I'll have to teach her to be more aware of her surroundings. Those two are idiots!*

Blake was about to get up and make her own lunch when the door opened again. She heard her Aunt Cinthia speaking as she came in. Gretel followed.

"I know you and Sage were off to the beach for the day, but before you go, I'd like to talk with you for a few minutes."

Gretel squirmed, and Blake recognized her friend's desire to be anywhere but with the coven leader. "That's fine, Cinthia. I don't mind postponing my day with Sage."

"Excellent." Aunt Cinthia walked into the kitchen and immediately saw Blake. "Oh, Blake, there you are. I was about to talk with Gretel. You're welcome to join us, but I know that you've been needing to research jobs in the area. We may be distracting."

Blake bit back a laugh at the look on her friend's face. She was also impressed with how completely she'd been dismissed by the coven leader. "I'll just head up to my room and continue my list of things to do while you have your talk with Gretel. Thanks for leaving the decision up to me."

Aunt Cinthia smiled. "Of course, dear. Lunch will be ready in twenty minutes."

Blake skipped up to her room, wondering what trouble her friend was in that warranted a twenty minute lecture from their leader. She snorted, deciding ignorance was better than getting involved.

CHAPTER 18 - YOU CUT A LOVELY FIGURE
Maria

Maria leaned back in the passenger seat of Georgette's car and shut her eyes. "This week has been too long. I'm so happy it's Friday." She rubbed her face, trying to wipe away the tension.

"Have you heard anything from the new wolf?"

"Blake? No. The Ferns? Yes. They should be arriving today."

Georgette made a happy sound. "That's not only two more wolves returning to the pack, it's Rainy. She's what, four?"

"Rainy is six, and I can't wait to play with her. Do you think she grew much in the last eight months?"

"Are you sure she's six? I could've sworn she was only four when she left."

"You're awful. She was five when she left, but her birthday is in March, so she's six. You can debate her age with her. I'm sure that will go over well."

Georgette laughed as she pulled into the garage. "Well, you can open up your eyes, trudge up to your room, and crash"

Stretching, Maria yawned. "No, I can't. I have a stupid-ass date tonight with one of those app people."

"You say that like they're all pod people."

"Well, it's kind of how it feels. The first two dates were busts." Maria pulled herself from the car and headed into the house. She heard talking in the living room and like a moth to flame, followed the commotion.

The Ferns had returned.

Jolly sat on one of the couches, looking tired. She'd tied back her brown hair and wisps were trying to escape, looking as bedraggled as her drooping body. Rainy slept across her lap. Timothy, Rainy's dad, slouched with his head lolled to one side. The light from the lamp next to him glared off his bald head and his mustache looked wild and unkempt.

Jolly gave her and Georgette a wan smile. "Hi, you two. It's so nice to see you."

Maria chuckled. "Why are you all up? You kind of look like the living dead. Go, take a nap."

"Mmmm," Timothy moaned. "Bed." He tried to straighten. "We were promised pizza, and the little one hasn't eaten. It'll be better if we get food into her first, then we collapse and play tomorrow. Tory isn't home, Connie's at work, and Orin is picking up the food."

"Will you join us?" Jolly asked, her smile brightening.

Georgette sat in the loveseat. "I will. Pizza sounds great." She pushed Maria towards the stairs. "This one has a date," she said in a singsong voice.

The other two lit up. Before they could ask any questions, Maria bolted to her room to get ready.

Nothing in her closet seemed appropriate for a date with a woman so ... exciting-looking. She decided to start with a cute bra and undies set. Not that she expected to get that far. But she had a few matching sets, and they made her feel sexy. *Why do romance authors always write about undies being ripped off? These things are expensive.*

She slipped the wine-colored set on, and felt more daring. She gazed at herself in the mirror, hands on her hips and smiled. "Well, Ms. Sanchez, don't you cut a lovely figure in this ensemble." She snorted at her own self-assessment.

She found a black cocktail dress in the back of her closet she forgot she owned. As she slid into it, she decided to leave her hair down. A bit of makeup, black flats, and she was ready to head out.

Skyler said she'd send the name of the restaurant where she wanted to meet. Maria hadn't checked the app at work because her day had been crazy. As she headed down the stairs, she finally opened the app and guffawed. From the living room, Georgette yelled, "Everything okay?"

"Yeah, Skyler chose Connie's restaurant. She even made reservations."

Maria headed to her car to a chorus of laughter.

Skyler wore a dark green skirt that barely covered ... anything. The outfit was sassy and alluring. Her skirt was paired with a cream wrap top blouse, covering the bits that needed to be covered. She had a belly-button ring that dangled a twinkling black jewel. Maria worried if the woman spun, her skirt would flare out, flat like a plate around her waist, revealing ... who knew what to the world.

Am I acting old? I should lighten up.

The other woman sauntered over to Maria and gazed down at her. Her bright green eyes sparkled in the evening light. "Hi, sexy Maria, I've been looking forward to meeting you."

Before Maria could answer, she slipped her hand behind Maria's head and pulled her in for a deep, searing kiss. Maria moaned as Skyler's free hand slid up her side and her thumb rubbed dangerously close to the tip of her breast. Maria reached out to clasp Skyler's hips and pull her closer.

After a few moments, Skyer pulled away. "Okay, yes. Perfect."

Maria shook her head. "What was that about?"

"I figure, get the first kiss out of the way right off the bat, and then we can focus on a good meal. If the kiss was a dud, we could cut our losses before spending the money. It's a win-win, really. So, lovely lady, shall we go order dinner? I'd really like to end the evening eating something good." Skyler smirked as she reached for Maria's hand.

Maria wondered if Skyler meant Connie's food, or something else, as they headed in for the reservation.

The meal was every bit as good as the last time Maria decided to spend half a paycheck at this restaurant. It wasn't *that* expensive, but almost. Skyler kept distracting her with her foot ... traveling ... upward. Chills ran up Maria's body as the foot played under her skirt.

Connie made an appearance. "I hear you two are out on a first date. I hope you enjoyed the meal."

Maria beamed up at her packmate, but Skyler took the lead. "The food was spectacular as always, Chef Connie. You run an excellent establishment here."

"I'm glad you appreciate it. In hopes that you two love-birds have success on future dates, the meal is on the house." Connie winked at Maria before turning and heading back into the kitchen.

A smile took over Skyler's face and she shimmied in her seat. "I've been coming here on and off for a few years, ever since I've moved here. I've heard Chef Connie sometimes gave out free meals, but I've never received one ... that was amazing." Her eyes sparkled with excitement. "Come on, let's go."

Maria held back, pulling her wallet from her purse.

Skyler looked at her, brows furrowed. "What are you doing?"

"Leaving a tip."

"But the meal, it was 'on the house.'" Skyler sounded utterly dumbfounded.

Maria sighed. "I still want to leave something for the staff, they shouldn't be stiffed. They were wonderful tonight. Don't worry, I've got it."

With a shrug, Skyler watched as Maria placed some bills on the table. She slipped her arm into Maria's, but it somehow didn't feel the way Maria wanted it to feel. Outside, Skyler asked, "Do you have a favorite beach? I thought we could sit and talk some more." She rubbed a hand up and down Maria's arm and gave her a hooded look. *Are those supposed to be bedroom eyes?*

A warmth infused Maria. Maybe the date was going better than she thought.

CHAPTER 19 - A PENDULUM - SWINGS BOTH WAYS
Blake

Friday morning came too soon. Blake had found an exotic dance club, and she had her interview this afternoon. She forced herself from bed and stumbled down to the kitchen for breakfast. For the first few days, Cinthia had helped out, but now that she and

Gretel had unpacked the moving van, they were on their own.

She found some dry oats and milk and set to making oatmeal. She turned on the coffee maker, then searched for accouterments: almonds, a bit of syrup, and golden raisins.

Once done eating, she quickly cleaned up, then went to shower and dress. The last time she'd interviewed at a strip club, she had to do a full show. She selected her black silk and lace undies and bra set, not the most comfortable, but easier than changing there. Thigh-high stockings with a garter belt, jeans, and a button-down shirt completed the look. Into her duffle she threw her leather slatted mini-skirt and heels. Sneakers were easier for walking.

The club was a couple of miles from her aunt's house. The day was beautiful, and the walk would do her good. She knew she'd probably have to break down and get a car sooner rather than later. But for now, the time outside would be perfect. The idea she could commute to work year round without a car thrilled her ... no blizzards here!

The establishment, Pendulum, was the only place Blake found in the area. She wasn't sure what to expect. Would it be the same as where she'd worked in Minnesota?

She pushed open the door and a man, ripped, oiled, and wearing a ... well, not a lot, walked by. A smile broke out on Blake's face. *Pendulum, it swings both ways. Oh, I'm going to like it here ... if I can get the job!*

She found L'Tisha, the manager, waiting for her at the bar. The woman's eyebrow rose, almost meeting her perfectly permed black and red cut hair. "There's a changing room in the back. You have five minutes, love. Then you have two hours—an hour on the floor, a slot on stage, then finish up on the floor. You'll keep your tips. Then the interview is over. After you change, return, and I'll give you a section."

Chills of anxiety mixed with excitement as Blake hurried off to the back. There was an empty locker with a key sticking out. She quickly changed, stashed her stuff, and put the key in her hip satchel, along with a pen, just in case.

Once back with L'Tisha, she was shown which tables she'd be running. She found an order pad and got to work.

At first, the rhythm was different than what she was used to in Minnesota, but she quickly felt the beat, and everything picked up. A table of men flirted with her, but they flirted amongst themselves more. A group of men and women could be there for the men or women. This job would be so much more thrilling than her old one. Anyone could be there for her to flirt with, and a few customers paid well for a lap dance with the new girl.

Her feet were sore after working for two hours. It was worth it, she'd made some good money. Not as much as the night shift, but better than nothing. L'Tisha said she'd done well, and a couple hours later, the paperwork was done. She got the job.

The walk home was unfortunate. Blake would need to figure out a better system for getting to and from work than walking, but free rent was hard to turn down.

When she got home, she took a long jacuzzi bath, then made spaghetti and meatballs for dinner. She hadn't expected Gretel to join her, and wasn't disappointed. She was just cleaning up when her 'roommate' walked in with her new best friend, Sage.

"Oh, if it isn't the wolf."

"Gretel, you've known me most of your life. What's your problem? Not to mention, you're living in *my* aunt's house!"

Sage mumbled behind Gretel, probably assuming it was too low for Blake to hear, "Her aunt's house? I thought it was the coven house."

"No, it's the coven's house—a witch house—and you're a werewolf." Gretel's face scrunched up in a sneer.

"For fuck's sake, Gretel, has anything about me changed? Like, really?"

Gretel's eyes narrowed and her hands balled on her hips. "Yes. You've lied to me, Blake. For over ten years, you've kept who you were from me. We were friends, I looked up to you, and what? Did you care? No, you lied. Why wasn't I good enough for you to tell me who you really were?"

Behind her, Sage tried to keep her face blank, but her mouth twitched as if she were fighting a smile.

Furry burned in Blake's gut, but she knew her friend hurt. *Why won't she talk to me like the friends we've been for half her life? What happened to the person I knew?* The anger won out. "Are you kidding me? The moment you found out, you spent the next week bad-mouthing me. The coven was all I had, Gretel. If they'd found out ... Gods above."

"What? What, Blake? You always have a pack, right?"

Tears stung Blake's eyes. "I wanted my friends. I didn't want to lose you, and Chey. Why can't you understand this? It's killing me to not have you in my life."

Gretel took Sage's hand, and snarled, good enough to be a wolf. "You should've thought about *that* before you lied."

Swallowing down her grief, she shook her head, and turned away from the contempt on Gretel's face. She focused on the floor as she passed the woman she thought she'd have in her life forever—until they were old and gray—and walked out the door.

She wasn't sure where she'd go. She picked a direction and hoped she could find her way back home later. Her feet were still sore, but what did it matter? Her heart hurt more. Blake decided to head towards the ocean. Watching the dark waves should calm her, if nothing else.

CHAPTER 20 - A BROKEN SET
Maria

The beach was close to the restaurant, so Maria and Skyler walked. A cool breeze came off the water, but the evening was warm. Maria took off her sandals and let the sand tickle her feet until they found a place to sit. They ended up close to the water.

Maria gazed out over the black waves, sparkling under the half moon and twinkling stars.

She sat with her knees up, leaning back on her hands. The bottom of her dress rode up her thighs, but it was too cold for that much skin to touch the chilled sand. Her gaze focused on the choppy waves. Next to her, Skyler's legs were stretched out towards the water. She leaned on one of her elbows, her other arm crossed over her waist.

Speaking softly, Maria asked, "Where did you live before you moved here?"

"To Santa Cruz? I moved here after college." Skyler moved her hand to Maria's knee. A shiver shot down her leg, pooling in a bit of heat in her gut. "Before college I lived in Oakland." Her warm hand moved down Maria's leg, fingers trailing along the inside of Maria's thigh. "How about you?"

Mouth dry, Maria tried to swallow. She took a ragged breath. All her focus remained on the hand slowly moving higher and higher up her leg. She tightened her lower muscles, anticipating the hand and what it might do when it reached its ultimate goal.

She looked over at Skyler and realized she'd moved closer and their faces were mere inches apart. "Um ... move here? I grew up here. I've always lived here."

"Hmm, interesting." Skyler leaned forward, closing the small distance between them, capturing Maria's mouth. Heat blossomed throughout Maria's body as Skyler's tongue began its assault.

Maria shifted to move her hand and Skyler pulled back. "Not this time. You stay just like that. Let me lead, okay? I'll tell you what I want."

The hand had reached its destination, and a single finger traced up and down the center of Maria's panties. The touch was feather-light, and it was driving Maria crazy. She felt herself grow wet with desire.

The finger began tracing circles. "Answer me, Maria. Do you agree?"

She nodded, not really knowing what she agreed to. The finger traced the edge of the panties and then she felt a jerk, and knew the woman had torn her undies. The pretty set was destroyed.

Maria pulled away as Skyler's hand reached and rubbed her most sensitive area. She gasped. "Did you just rip my undies off?"

"Hot, right? I wanna tear off all your clothes and devour you, sexy woman."

"But not really, right?"

Skyler leaned in and pushed Maria down. "I don't know. You naked and at my mercy sounds divine. When we get home, I'll include some handcuffs and a whip, then we'll really have some fun. You're all wet down here." Skyer thrusted two fingers in Maria, hard and sudden. "I know you want it." Her mouth fell on Maria's in a demanding kiss.

A wave of disgust consumed Maria. She tried to push away, but Skyler pinned Maria down, thrusting her fingers in and out and deepening the kiss.

With a low snarl, Maria pushed the other woman off. Skyler flew back, landing on her butt. Being smaller than Skyler, the other woman's face mimicked the emoji with wide eyes and an open mouth of shock at the power of the thrust.

Maria growled, "I think the date's over."

"What? I know you want me."

"No, Skyler, I don't. Good-bye."

"Come back, do as I say."

Maria clenched her fists as she stomped towards her car. Another date, another failure, and this one ended in a lost pair of undies left on the beach for someone to find.

CHAPTER 21 - MAYBE MEET SOMEONE ON THE BEACH
Blake

The walk to the beach was therapeutic. Her first week in Santa Cruz, Blake had sent Chey a couple of text messages asking her friend to call, but she only received a single text back.

Gretel told me about what happened. Give me some time to figure some things out.

Blake figured the rest of her old coven knew by now, and didn't even try to contact any of them. She wasn't sure where she fit in anymore. Aunt Cinthia accepted her, but she wasn't sure about the rest of the coven. Aunt Cinthia wanted her to come to a coven meeting on Sunday afternoon. She was still debating if she wanted to face the firing squad.

Turning a random corner, she saw a beach. She hoped she'd be able to find her way back home. *If it wasn't as windy, or I wanted to smell the ground, I could follow my own scent back, but I like these clothes and I don't want to travel as a wolf. If nothing else, I'll map it on my phone. How sad is that? What did people do before smartphones?*

The beach was a dark smudge and the moon shone off dark waves sparkling with the stars above. It matched her roiling mood. At first, she thought the sandy plane was empty, but then she saw a paired silhouette near the water. With a shrug, she sat on the edge of the beach. She didn't want to interrupt the romantic duo;

she just wanted to be alone. No one seemed to want her, anyway.

Is that fair? That Orin guy wasn't accepting, but Maria and the rest of the pack seemed to be. So, like Aunt Cinthia and the witches, part of the coven sees me as a witch, to the rest, I'm just a freak. Will I ever find my place now that my secret's out?

Blake stretched her legs out and tried to let the vastness of the ocean calm her.

"No, Skyler, I don't. Goodbye." Was that Maria's voice? Blake tried to catch her scent on the air, but the wind wasn't in her favor.

"Come back. Do as I say."

Oh, no. That other woman is a demanding bitch. Unless the two are like that, but the first doesn't sound like she's enjoying the game.

Blake sat up, debating what to do when the first woman started walking towards her. As she got closer, Blake pulled on her wolf and her night vision improved. The details cleared, and she made out the specific shape and swing of the hip. *Holy hell, that's Maria!*

Behind her, another woman scrambled to her feet. She was a bit taller and a knock-out. *Is that Maria's type? No wonder she never called. No, wait. That isn't fair.*

The knock-out followed. She didn't move as fast as Maria, but she looked like she wanted to catch up and continue whatever they'd started. When Maria got close enough, Blake made up her mind. She spoke softly, but wolves had amazing hearing. "Maria, it's Blake. Join me?"

The other woman paused in her flight. Her head snapped left, then right, before she found Blake sitting in the sand. After a few seconds, her head jerked down in a quick nod, then she made her way to Blake and sat down. "What are you doing here?"

"I needed space to think."

"Do you want to be alone? I can leave."

Blake hooked her arm in Maria's and enjoyed the tingles that engulfed her body she was coming to expect with the woman. "No, stay. Please."

The other woman had finally caught up. Her face was screwed up tight and her hands were on her hips. She finally spat out. "What are you doing? Who is this?"

Blake looked up. *She might be a knock-out, but from the way Maria's acting, she's also a bad date.* She smiled. "I'm the other woman, of course." She slipped her hand around Maria's neck and pulled her in for a kiss. Gods, how she'd wanted to do this. If there were any resistance, she would stop. There wasn't. Blake's lips met Maria's in what Blake planned on being a chaste kiss.

Without thinking, her tongue darted out for a quick taste. Maria gasped, and Blake deepened the kiss. Maria matched her stroke for stroke. Her hand slid over to Blake's hip as the kiss continued. Heat began to boil in Blake's gut as every instinct told her to keep going. It may be a public beach, but it was dark, they were alone ... mostly.

With a moan, Blake pulled away. They both remained close, breathing roughly, gazing into each other's eyes.

A low growl came from Maria as she leaned forward, then paused. She shot a look over her shoulder. Blake followed and saw the other woman had left. Maria scrunched up her face and moved away. "Thank you."

Blake wanted to pull her close and finish what they'd started but worried if she did, it would just be something to erase a bad date. Blake wanted it to be more. "Of course."

Maria scooted over, leaning back on her hands, knees up. "Why is dating so hard?"

"Maybe you're looking in the wrong places."

"Where do people even go to find dates in this day and age? This app is a complete bust."

Blake huffed out a laugh and let her head fall back. "If we were in Minnesota, I'd say the bar. But here in Santa Cruz, I don't know, maybe the beach?"

Maria, her gaze glued to the water, shrugged. "Maybe. Usually it's families and tourists, but that's an idea. I just ... why can't it just be someone presented to me on a silver platter?"

"Would you notice if it were?"

"Probably not. I need someone to just tell me we're dating and that's that. There's so much going on with work and the pack. I probably should've told Georgette that I needed to wait until after Tamsin got back before I started dating again."

"So, are you going to stop going on these dates then?" Blake hoped she didn't hear the note of desperation in her voice. She wasn't sure she'd do anything about her own feelings, but if Maria continued going on dates, then she'd eventually find someone who wasn't crazy … and that person would realize how amazing Maria was.

"I don't know. I have to think about it." Maria sighed. "So, enough about my sucky night. Think you'll ever come back to the pack?"

"Do you think they want me?" Blake's shoulders hunched in and she pulled her knees up to hug them. She realized the ocean's turbulence matched her emotions perfectly.

Maria darted a look at Blake before her gaze returned to the water. "Some of us do."

Warmth flowed through Blake's body. "And the others?"

"We'll beat Orin into submission." She said it with a small laugh. "I don't even know what's wrong with him."

"I'm having the same issue with my coven friends. Tell you what, whoever figures it out first lets the other one know, agreed?"

Maria leaned over and briefly rested her forehead on Blake's shoulder. "It's a deal."

CHAPTER 22 - CAN'T BE WORSE!
Maria

"**A**nyone want coffee or tea?" Connie's voice pulled Maria from the rich fantasy world of magic and intrigue.

She closed *Heliacle Rising,* one of her favorite books. She'd read it enough times the binding was getting thin. She checked the time.

Noon. How had it gotten to be so late? "Connie, when did you get up? I'll take some tea, thanks."

The others sitting around the room put in their orders. An even mix of tea and coffee, and one request for juice.

Connie poked her head out from the kitchen. "It's noon, Maria, of course I'm up. Can you come in and help me with this? I can't carry everything myself, and I have something to discuss with you."

"Sure." She ambled up, not sure if she was excited to talk to the older packmate.

In the kitchen, they put together two trays, one with the coffee, the tea in a pot to steep, and a pitcher of orange juice. The other had a few glasses, mugs, sugar, and milk.

Before they could carry their loads out, Connie put a hand on Maria's arm to stop her. "Can we hold a moment? I'd like to ask you about your date last night. It went well, right?"

Maria scowled. "It started okay but no. I won't be seeing her again." Maria sat hard on one of the kitchen chairs. "I just don't think I'm ready for the dating world. Why?"

Connie sat next to her. "Huh, the two of you seemed to be getting along well. Juniper, your waitress, you know her, she thought you two were a great couple."

"I love Juniper." Maria smiled, thinking of the woman. "She and her girlfriend have been together for a long time, right? Relationship goals."

Connie laughed. "No, they'd been doing great until her girlfriend got it in her head to become an actress and moved to L.A. They haven't been together in over a year. You're very behind in the gossip. Anyway, I guess Juniper has had a crush on you for a while and was hoping to go on a date with you when she heard you were finally dating. Then when she saw you out last night ... well she decided it was too late."

Maria thought about the waitress with the strawberry blond curls and pale blue eyes, and smiled. She'd known Juniper for a few years. The woman wasn't crazy, or weird, at least not in a bad or scary way. "Well, I was thinking about giving up on dating again ..."

"Why not give her a call? You know our schedule is stupid busy, but maybe brunch tomorrow?"

"Fine, give me her number. I'll give it a shot. It can't be worse than the last three dates I went on."

Maria got to the Brunch Stop before Juniper. She couldn't believe she was going on another date. This would be three in a week. Then again, this time it was with someone she knew ... sort of. At least Juniper wasn't crazy.

She saw Juniper approach wearing black slacks and a nice, light blue top. The two hugged before heading in. Once seated, Maria asked, "Do you ever find it weird being waited on by other people? Do you judge the service? Or do you just enjoy not having to be the one working?"

Juniper laughed, and it was a good laugh. "Honestly, I try to separate myself from work when I'm out, especially with someone so lovely." She blushed. "It's hard not to be critical, but I'm out to enjoy myself and being judgmental isn't fun."

"I agree." Maria tentatively placed her hand out on the table palm up, a bit further out than normal. Juniper gazed at it for a moment, then gently placed her hand on top.

She waited for tingles, but they didn't come. She shook her head. *Don't fret about it, Maria. You're out with a beautiful woman who seems semi-normal, so enjoy yourself.*

Smiling, Maria turned to the menu to figure out what she wanted to order. She tried not to dwell on the tingles she longed for. *I did have them last night in that searing kiss ... Gods above, that kiss! No, stop thinking about locking lips with Blake!*

She couldn't have anything with Blake ... could she? She was out with a lovely woman, and she was going to have a good time.

CHAPTER 23 - NOTHING THAT BELONGS TO YOU IS INSIGNIFICANT
Blake

Blake sat on the edge of her bed and debated what to do. The coven meeting started in a half hour. She could head out and find a coffee shop, get something to eat, sit at a library and read, explore Santa Cruz ...

so many options. Did she want to let a group of women she didn't know judge her?

A knock jolted her from her thoughts. "Um, yeah, come in."

The door opened and a woman with frizzy auburn hair and bright green eyes poked her head in. Blake narrowed her eyes and realized she recognized the woman—this was the one who had outed her as a wolf. Scowling, she asked, "What do you want?"

The other woman came in and shut the door. "Hi, my name is Fiona—Fe—and I wanted to apologize to you." She leaned against the door. "I didn't mean to tell your secret to anyone. I didn't realize it *was* a secret. I've never met a wolf who hid their nature. I've also never met a wolf who was also a witch." She pushed off the wall and approached the bed. She stopped half way and gave a small smile. "Our coven meetings are always closed and private. I thought you were one of Tamsin's wolves here to pick up something of hers. My question was rude ... I'm often rude, but legit. I didn't know why a wolf was at a coven meeting."

Blake lifted her feet to the bed, crossing her ankles and hugging her knees. "That's all fine and good, but that leaves me unwelcome. I've hidden who I was because the witches don't allow wolves, and wolves don't allow witches. I'm now without a group or a pack—not that I've ever had a pack—and I'm not sure what to do or where to go."

"Who said you couldn't be part of our coven?" Fe tilted her head as she sat on the end of the bed, brow creased.

Blake rested her cheek on her knees. "I just ... everyone gaped at me with so much animosity last week. And everyone from my old coven always seemed very anti-wolf."

Fe's eyes widened. "Everyone?"

"Well, I've only really talked to Gretel and another friend. It's just ... I feel like I'm being removed like an unwanted mistake. It hurts." She felt a tear on her cheek and she quickly wiped it away. "I don't want to be included if I'm not wanted. I just need to figure out where to go."

Fe sat down next to her and put a hand on her shoulder. "You are a witch, right?"

Blake nodded, her body tensing with pent up emotion. Her belly tightening, a knot formed in her throat, and more tears gathering in her eyes.

"And you can do magic?" Fe continued.

Blake slowly relaxed the muscles in her right arm, turned out her hand, palm up, and focused, creating a ball of green flames. On an exhale, her magic dissipated.

Fe's hand rubbed across her shoulders until the other woman held her in a half hug. "Then you belong with us, my friend. We look at the magic. We don't care if there's more. You can work with plants, right? With the intensity of that green, you're obviously very good. I can't see the color of the magic as well as I see animals. As you may have guessed, my strength is animals, though I'm good with water magic as well. Do you have a second proficiency, or is it all plants?"

No one had ever asked her that; they'd all always assumed she only could work with plants. She held out her hand again and the green flame shot up. With a push, a tiny yellow streak wound around the outside of the green like a ribbon around a gift. It was small, but there.

Fe gazed at it. "That must be connected to your werewolf side. I can work with you on developing that ... if you want."

"I would. I've never shown anyone I had anything but plant magic ... it seemed insignificant."

"Nothing that belongs to you is insignificant, Blake, that's the first rule around here. Now, come, meet the others, and join the coven. It's time to start doing some magic." Fe stood and wrapped an arm around Blake's shoulder with a smile.

Chills suffused her body followed by a warmth of acceptance as she followed the fiery young witch down the stairs. This time when she looked at the other women in the room, she didn't see animosity or hate; she saw other women interested in who she was. Well, she saw a bit of doubt from Gretel, but she could work with that.

CHAPTER 24 - A GAGGLE OF GOSSIP
Maria

The car ride home from work Monday had been silent ... too silent. Maria was suspicious of Georgette when she didn't have a million things to say. When they got into the house, she was about to head up to her room for a few minutes of solitude when her friend clasped her forearm. "Wanna sit for a few minutes in the living room? Unwind together?"

"We had the whole drive home and now you want to talk?" Maria eyed her friend with the trust she deserved.

Georgette stared back, one eyebrow raised.

"Fine, sure, a few minutes. Then I'm heading up to be alone."

In the living room, Jolly sat in the recliner with Rainy playing in the corner and Orin lounged on a couch, reading. Jolly gazed up at them. "Timothy is off to the local Thai restaurant that he's been fantasizing about since we left and getting enough food to feed an army. It may even be enough for tonight."

Maria snorted as she sat.

Georgette, as usual, took a spot next to her. "So, three dates last week. How were they?"

"Really, you want to talk about it now, with everyone here?" Dread surged through her. She knew she wasn't avoiding this conversation.

"Why not?"

Maria searched Jolly's face, passed over Orin, gazed at Rainy, and finally looked at Georgette. "It's ... personal."

"We live in a pack. It either comes from you directly, or it gets mangled through gossip." Jolly laughed. "I remember my dating days. You may as well do it here and now." She rubbed Rainy's back. "Rainy, love, can you bring those toys up to your room and play up there until Dad gets back? We're going to talk about adult stuff."

Rainy flopped to her back. "That's so boring, Mom. Gah!" She jumped up, picked up one toy, and darted away.

Maria waited until she heard a door close upstairs. "Okay, I'm not getting into any details. Rose, the date Monday, wanted to see what dating women was like ... just no. I won't be a test run. Skyler—" Maria rolled her eyes. "She wants a play toy, and was aggressive about it."

The shocked faces around the room annoyed Maria, but she understood their concern.

Georgette placed her hand on Maria's leg. "Are you okay?"

"Yes I'm okay. We're werewolves. No human can successfully pin me down. Not to mention, she did it at the beach, and when I stormed off, I ran into Blake. She and I pretended to be an item, and that finally convinced Skyler to leave."

Georgette's brow lifted again. "Pretended?"

Maria huffed. "Yes, pretended. Then we sat and talked for a bit." Maria turned. "Orin, you need to figure out your reason for being anti-witch. Blake is a good person *and* a wolf. She needs a pack. She needs us. She's a really good person ... and ... I like her. And I don't know why someone who's always been so nice has suddenly become an ass."

He glared at Maria. "She's a witch first. You saw where her priorities lie. We can't trust her."

"What are you even talking about? Trust her. What's she going to do? Tell the witches we turn into wolves? We run under the moon? What are you scared of?"

"Just stay away from her!" His mouth pressed into a line as he crossed his arms over his chest.

"What the fuck, Orin? Since when do you tell me what to do?"

"Obviously someone needs to, with you going around making out with her on the beach in the middle of the night."

Jolly laughed and everyone turned to her. "We don't know what they did on the beach, but if Maria has a connection with this Blake person, I personally support it. Orin, your beliefs are out of date ... and wrong. But we're getting caught up on the end of the second date. Wasn't there a third?"

Maria realized her nails were biting into her palms, and worked to relax her fingers. "Yes, there was. Connie set me up with one of the waitresses from her restaurant. Juniper. She's nice. We actually have a second date scheduled for Thursday. She works a lot, but has Thursday night off."

Orin, still with a sour face, grumbled, "Good. Hopefully she'll get the witch out of your system."

Maria opened her mouth to answer when her phone rang. Checking the display, she saw it was Tamsin. "Hello, oh fearless leader, I have you on speaker. There are several of us here and listening."

"Excellent, then I know fewer will get the message mangled." Everyone chuckled. "I've been doing a lot of research to help us figure out what to do about Blake."

Georgette leaned forward. "Any conclusions?"

"Not exactly. Though I think I know what I want to do. I'd like to meet her first. This school year can't end soon enough."

"You're telling me," Paige grumbled from the background.

There was a pause before Tamsin continued. "Did you know that a black witch coven broke up a wolf pack in South Dakota?"

Jolly sat up. "The pack we joined? When we left, they hinted at it. It had happened long enough ago that not many had good details. It was why the current pack and local coven got along so well. The witches and wolves had to work together to get rid of them. Ever since, the two groups have worked in harmony. Better than we do here."

"That's what I've been learning. It's the same in Chicago and with the other packs that helped break up the kerfuffle. Anyway, I just wanted to get you all up to speed with what I'm learning. Jolly, can you fill them in on the rest of the situation?"

"Can do, boss."

Tamsin laughed as she signed off.

Orin scowled. "I still don't like this." Throwing his book on the couch, he stomped up the stairs.

Georgette gazed at her hands. "If you like Juniper, that's great, Maria. But your eyes shine when you speak of Blake. Really think about what you want, my friend." Then she, too, got up and headed up the stairs, leaving Maria with Jolly.

Before anything else was said, Tory came in, a bundle of happy energy. "Honeys, I'm home, did I miss anything?"

CHAPTER 25 - COME TO YOUR SENSES, YOUNG ONE
Blake

Wednesday afternoon, Blake lounged on the couch reading a book.

The coven agreed she could remain living at the house for as long as she needed. It was a bonus, having someone live in the house, maintain the building, and always have it ready for the meetings. When they'd bought it, they'd wanted a coven member who could relocate, but everyone else already had a place to live. For them, this was ideal. So, it seemed her living situation was set.

The next big obstacle Blake needed to figure out was what she wanted to do about the pack. Right now, she was pretty sure an 'avoid at all costs' policy seemed best. She'd been doing that all her life, and if it wasn't broke, then why fix it?

Maria—that's why, fool!

She closed her eyes, thought about the wolf, and sighed. She didn't know what she wanted to do about the other woman.

Footsteps on the stairs alerted her of Gretel's approach. Blake tensed and put the book down. *Ugh. I'm not up for another fight.*

"Hi, Blake. Can we talk?"

Blake's muscles tightened more, if that was possible. "Can we not?" Her words came out rough and low. She wasn't up to battling her friend today.

Gretel held up her hands as she approached. "I know; I've been a bitch. I don't want to head off to college with us like this. Please, let me apologize."

Narrowing her eyes, Blake followed the other woman's movements as she took a seat on the couch across from her. Gretel leaned forward. "I'm moving out this weekend. June is around the corner and I'm moving closer to campus."

"Do you have to? Won't it be expensive?" *Why am I trying to keep her here? It'll mean the continuation of living in a hostile environment.*

"I just ... I didn't want to take advantage."

Blake sighed. "Did anyone say you had to?"

"Well, no. But I figured they'd want me out of here, that's all."

Blake rubbed her face. "There are four rooms up there, not to mention the master down here. If we both live here, three other people can still visit. I doubt the coven plans on having that many visitors."

"But would you want to live with me, given how I've been acting?"

"As you and Sage keep reminding me, it isn't my decision. And how about you? Would you want to live with a werewolf?"

She let her head drop. "If it's you, then yes. I ... Blake, I was hurt. I don't know why I wasn't thinking about you and what you were going through. Cinthia finally sat me down and made me think about it. It wasn't that you hadn't told me; you hadn't told *anyone*. And the first thing I did was exactly what you feared. I wasn't the friend I should've been. I can't erase the last week, but I'm hoping to make it up. I know you, and I want to continue being your friend. I miss you ... us ... our friendship."

Blake smiled. "Thank the gods. The thought of losing you, and Chey, and everything. I was losing my mind."

"Well, I don't know about Chey, but it'll take more than that to lose me."

It felt like a weight lifted from her shoulders. "Good."

"So, tell me about the wolf who's been introducing you to pack life ... this Maria?"

Blake blushed. She didn't think most people would notice, but this was Gretel.

Gretel's eyes widened. "Oh, my Gods, you like her!"

They spent the next few minutes catching up on the last week and everything that had happened. At the end, Gretel's nose scrunched up and she smiled mischievously. "Call her. Call her—here and now. Ask her out on a date."

"What?" A pit formed in Blake's stomach.

"Do it!"

Shaking, Blake patted her pockets to find her phone, but before she could do anything, a knock sounded on the door.

Saved by the ... door, Blake leapt up and headed to the entrance. "Ah ... maybe later. I'll think about it."

Gretel's voice followed her from around the corner. "You will call Maria, Ms. Blake, and you *will* ask her out. You owe it to both of you!"

Not daring to answer, Blake reached out and opened the door. She gaped. "Mom! What are you doing here?"

"I wanted to help you figure all this out. Thirty years hiding from the covens and now this? How are you doing?"

Blake led her into the living room and her mom gazed coldly at Gretel. Her friend stood and approached. "Hi, Ms. Dillon. I know you probably heard horrible things, but I've apologized. I've missed you these last few years you've been away. Could I ... um ... could I get a hug?"

Mom's face relaxed, but only a pinch. She looked down at Gretel, then stepped forward and pulled the woman in for a hug. "I'm glad you came to your senses, young one. Hearing about the split between the two of you didn't sit well with me."

"I know, it didn't feel good—in here." Gretel rubbed her chest. "I just ... I needed to get my head on right."

They sat next to each other on a couch and Blake scrunched up her face. "But, Mom, what are you doing here?"

"Haven't you learned anything? Now that you're out, wolves need a pack ... and family. If you're going to be running as a wolf—in a pack— I'd like to run with you. I've missed that. I'm going to go talk to that pack and their alpha, see what it'll take to join."

Blake leaned back. "The alpha isn't here. She's in Chicago until the end of the school year."

"Well, then, we'll have to go speak with the rest of the pack and see if I like them. If I do, then I can interview the head honcho."

Blake laughed. Her mother always had such a different take on things.

CHAPTER 26 - THERE WEREN'T ANY TINGLES
Maria

As Georgette drove home, Maria watched the homes fly by. She was nervous about a second date with Juniper. The woman was pretty and nice. None of her other dates had gotten to the second date. "Where did you go, Maria?"

Shaking her head, Maria let her eyes blur as she tried to concentrate on her friend's words. "I'm sorry. Did you ask me something?"

"Are you excited about your date tonight?"

"Yes ... I mean, she's really nice. Why wouldn't I be?"

"I don't know—you tell me. You've been quiet for days."

Maria slumped. "I don't know. The first date was ... nice."

"You keep saying that. Is 'nice' enough?"

"Shouldn't it be?"

"I'm not you, my friend. You tell me."

"There weren't any tingles with Juniper. She's sweet and pretty, and our conversation was fun ... but I miss the tingles."

Georgette's brows came together as her face scrunched. "You lost me, Maria. 'The tingles'? Can you elaborate?"

Maria blew out a gush of air, puffing her bangs off her forehead. "You know, when you touch someone. Like, hold hands, and you feel tingles."

Georgette's eyes softened. "Oh, dear. You have it bad for Blake, don't you? Why are you denying it?"

"What? No. I mean, yeah, it does happen with her, but that isn't what I was talking about."

"Why aren't you going on a date with her?"

"I don't know. If she becomes part of the pack and we date and it's a disaster ... it'll be so awkward. I like her, and I want our relationship to be a good one—not the awkwardness of stilted exes maneuvering around each other."

"You're thinking too hard. Just go on a date and see what happens. If your wolves have decided they're compatible—and the humans like each other—then any other pairing will just leave the two of you miserable. You know that."

"You think our wolves have decided?"

Georgette's eyes slid to her before focusing back on the road. "I don't know, but the two of you are certainly acting ... connected. I think it would be short-sighted to not give this a chance just because you're worried about the pack. You could be missing out on an opportunity for happiness, and I would hate for that to happen. You need to be selfish in this."

"You're assuming she wants to date a dumpy woman six years older than her."

Maria jerked forward as Georgette slapped her upside the head. "Do not disparage your curvaceous body. You're beautiful, not dumpy. Have any of your dates complained?"

"Well, no."

"So, don't. Just ... don't."

"Fine." Maria rolled her eyes at the woman who was so like a sister. Georgette always knew exactly what to say to break her out of her funk.

They pulled into the garage and Maria headed up to her room to change for her date. Despite what Georgette thought, she knew dating Blake came with risks—and that was *if* Blake wanted to date.

She took a quick shower and slipped on a pale yellow dress. She and Juniper were heading out to a seafood restaurant. The night was chilly, so she grabbed a charcoal-gray shawl before driving to the restaurant.

Okay, last time the date was merely okay because it was brunch on a Sunday. This time the date will be better. We're going out at night, Juniper is beautiful, we're both excited. I'm sure we'll have the tingles. I was just tired and not paying attention. Tonight will be our night.

Juniper arrived almost at the same time wearing a green dress that sparkled in the light. She looked lovely. Again they hugged, and this time they kissed cheeks. No fireworks yet, but the night was young, there was time. They were seated at a table by the window with a white tablecloth and a fake candle in the center. Juniper ordered wine while they looked over the menu.

Juniper smiled. "Do you know what you want?"

"I do. How about you?"

"I'm ready." She folded up her menu and set it down. "How was your day?"

"Good. I'm working on this project with this group to set up a new router and set up their new website for a business. They had a store where they sold their goods, but no welcome page, no protections. It's insane what people think is safe on the internet." Maria chuckled as she noticed Juniper checking out her nails, then the restaurant's decor. "I'm sorry, you probably think this is boring. From the outside, it's pretty monotonous, but from my side it's all puzzles and adventures."

Juniper picked up her wine and took a healthy drink. "Oh, no—it's great. I love hearing about what you do. So, you built a wall of fire? Is that safe? Are there fire extinguishers in your office?" Her eyes were wide, but her voice was a bit too bright, as if she were trying too hard to sound interested, though Maria could tell she wasn't.

Maria nodded a bit sadly. She thought about changing the subject, but wanted to answer her question. "Something like that. What do you do with your phone? Do you have a computer?"

The other woman shrugged, ducking down. "Oh, you know, social media mostly. I like to read books. I play games, too. I have a laptop at home, but to be honest, I don't really use it much. I use my phone for most things."

The waitress came and took their order. After she left, Maria picked up the thread of their small talk.

"Did you go to school before working for Connie?"

"Oh, yeah, I graduated from Santa Cruz high."

"How old are you? Did we attend at the same time?"

Juniper blushed. "We did. You were a senior my freshmen year. I'm thirty-three. I remember you, but I wouldn't expect you to remember me. I was pretty quiet. I heard you went off to college in Stanford. After I graduated, I got jobs around town until I figured out I was really good at service." She ducked her head with a small smile. "I like what I do."

She spent a few minutes telling a few tales about the different jobs she'd held over the years. The food was delivered and they ate while they shared a few laughs.

"That's excellent. Nothing wrong with doing what you love. That's what my mom used to tell me. Figure out what you love to do, then find a way to get paid to do it."

She beamed. "I love that. Does your mom still live around here?"

Maria sat back, not ready for the question that hit her like a punch in the gut. When Vernon took over the pack late the previous year, many wolves left. Her parents were two of them. They headed east. Her father had a run-in with a crazy lone wolf, and neither of her parents survived. They'd been traveling with another couple from the pack, and they'd sent word so Maria knew she was now alone in the world.

A hand rubbed her arm.

Maria realized she'd zoned out remembering her family. She'd lost the thread of the conversation and gazed blankly at Juniper.

The other woman's face softened. "I'm sorry. I don't know what I said or what happened, but I'm really sorry."

Maria shook her head. "It isn't you. I've just avoided thinking about it … about them. There was an accident last year. They didn't survive. I'm sorry. This evening has been lovely, but I don't know that I'll be any more fun. I probably should go soon."

Juniper nodded. "I get it. You're still processing it all. I've had a really good time with you. I was hoping—"

Maria stood and tossed money on the table. She leaned down and kissed Juniper's cheek. Nothing. No tingles, no chills, no goosebumps or thrills. She bit back a sigh. "Good night, Juniper."

She turned from the table and made her way to her car. With every fiber in her body, she'd hoped the night would be spectacular.

It wasn't.

CHAPTER 27 - A WELL BALANCED MEAL
Blake

"Pass the chips." Blake looked at her lunch, deciding what else she wanted to add.

Gretel tossed one in her mouth before passing the bowl. "This is the best lunch idea ever."

Mom rolled her eyes. "You two are too old to be eating like this."

"Do you want a shell to build yours in, or just a bowl?" Blake waggled her eyebrows as she waved a fried bowl in one hand and a porcelain one in the other.

Her mom snatched the fried one. "If you're going to be moronic imbeciles during a meal, why waste time on something like that?" She waved her spoon at the offending porcelain bowl.

Gretel laughed. "Okay, we have chocolate marshmallow swirl, vanilla monkey tracks—which have peanut butter cups and caramel swirls—and pistachio surprise."

Mom looked at the three flavors of ice cream. "What's the surprise?"

Blake grabbed the container. "White chocolate chunks, and no actual pistachios." Blake grinned.

Eyes narrowed, Mom examined the toppings Blake and Gretel had gathered for the ice cream lunch creations. There were different flavored chips, syrups, sprinkles, and, of course, whipped cream. Blake knew they'd all end up sick, but it'd be worth it.

"Hand over the pistachio surprise, white chocolate chips, pistachios, and marshmallow syrup."

Once their bowls of devilishly good creations were constructed, they started to eat.

"So, Blake, have you called Maria yet?" Gretel waved her spoon covered in chocolate ice cream at her, eyes squinting, as if she could read Blake's mind.

If her stare could fry her friend where she sat, Gretel wouldn't have to worry about classes starting up in a few days.

Gretel snorted. "We talked about this, like, a week ago. Your mom's been here for over a week—"

"Only just a week, dear, but you were close." Mom said, taking another bite of her outlandish lunch.

"Fine, a week. It's been a week, Blake. Have you called Maria like you said you would?"

Mom waved her spoon at Blake. "Who is Maria?"

Slumping in her chair, Blake felt defeated. "When I first arrived, the pack assigned a wolf to show me around, to make me feel welcome."

"And it was this Maria lady?"

"Yes, Mom."

"And why do you need to call her? Do you need help with the pack? Have they been derelict in their duties?"

She growled softly. "No, it's nothing like that. Well, not really. One of the pack members, Orin, has a real stick up his ass against witches, but the rest of the pack seems to be okay. But ..." Blake trailed off. *How do I explain this without Mom teasing me as much as Gretel?*

"Blake has a crush on Maria," Gretel said in a sing-song voice, smiling mischievously.

Her mom smiled back. "Do you, now? Tell me about it."

"Gah! Mother!"

"This could be important, sweetie. Humor me."

Blake dropped her head onto her folded arms and groaned. "I don't know. When we first met ... I've never had it happen before. It was like an instant connection. She's nice and fun to talk to, but there was something there before I even knew her." Blake's face heated.

Her mom reached over and rubbed her arm. "Did I ever tell you some wolves connect with others?"

Blake's head popped up. "Like a mate?"

Gretel smiled. "You're living in your own romance."

"Stop, you dork!" She threw a chocolate chip at her friend as they both burst out in laughter.

After they calmed down, Blake asked, "So, a connection like you and Dad?"

"No. I loved your dad, don't get me wrong, but there are stories of wolves who were connected who can't survive without each other. When one dies, the other dies shortly thereafter. It hurt losing your dad, but I still wanted to live."

On the other side of the table, Gretel watched as if a great drama played out, eating her ice cream. She finally put down her spoon. "Personally, I'm glad you lived, but we need to not let her distract us." She shifted her focus to Blake. "Make the call."

"Yes, dear," her mom agreed. "Make the call."

Patting down her body as if she were frisking herself, she almost declared she didn't have a phone, but then she felt it in her back pocket. *Damn it!*

She glared at Gretel as she made a show of pulling out her phone, finding the contacts, and selecting Maria. As soon as the line started to ring, she jerked and put the phone to her ear, forgetting it was more than for show.

"Hello? Blake?"

"Oh. Hi." Blake stood and walked into the master bedroom, shutting the door behind her. "How are you?"

"Um, good. Work's good. Home's good. Things are ..."

Blake laughed as she sat on the bed. "Good?"

"Well, yeah. I guess I'm kind of boring."

"I don't think you're boring. Any more amazingly bad dates?"

"No. Well, yes, bad. Just not 'lose your underwear' bad."

Blake's jaw dropped. "You were sitting next to me on the beach without underwear on?"

Maria chuckled, low and husky. "Maybe."

Blake bit back a moan as heat pooled below her belly. "I can't believe I didn't know."

She heard a door close across the line. "Would you have done anything different had you known?"

Blake wanted to purr. "Maybe, but now we'll never know."

A soft chuckle. "What's a girl to do?"

"We could have a redo. You and me—dinner Friday night. No undies allowed." Blake bit her lip and waited, hoping.

Finally, Blake heard Maria take a deep breath. "Friday night? Okay. Like a date?"

"Yes, a date. You, me, dinner ... and don't forget the no undies ... that part is very important." Her heart pounded in her chest, she couldn't believe Maria said yes, and she'd made the silly demand.

Maria laughed. "So, how was your day? Are you keeping busy?"

"I am. I got a job, I have this beautiful house to live in, and my Mom is here visiting." She rolled her eyes that a job and Mom made her top three, but talking to Maria put her at ease.

"Your mom? Is she going to come visit the pack?"

"Not even one date and you're ready to meet the parents? You *do* move fast."

"Well, you know what a lesbian brings to the second date."

They both said together, "A moving van!"

A pounding shook the door. "Blake, your lunch is melting."

She groaned. "Maria, I have to go. Lunch with Mom and Gretel. But Friday. How about Thai?"

"Mmm, sounds perfect." Gods above, the sounds Maria made *did* things to her. "Do you want me to pick you up since I have a car and know where you live?"

"Yes, Ms. Stalker, sounds perfect." Her voice was huskier than when they'd started their conversation. She wondered if Maria noticed.

Shutting her phone, her insides buzzed with anticipation. She couldn't believe how excited she was for her date. *Why did I wait so long to make this call?*

CHAPTER 28 - GOBSMACKED
Maria

Most days, Maria wore dresses. She had a closet full of them. A full rainbow of colors and styles that she thought she looked pretty decent in. The thought of wearing a dress that could fly up ... and if she followed through with not wearing undies. Maria gulped.

What the hell am I thinking? Am I really going to do this? It's absolutely bonkers! Every bit of it, from going on a date with Blake, to even considering her dress code requirement. Gah! Am I daft?

Searching her dresser, she found a cute scoop-neck shelf tank in a rich dark blue that buttoned behind her neck. She put it on, then secured and adjusted it to make sure it covered and supported as she remembered. The bottom skimmed the top of her belly button, barely decent. In another drawer, she found a high-waisted cream skirt that buttoned down the front. It went from below her belly button to halfway to her knees, hugging her hips.

In front of a mirror, she applied minimal makeup and pinned up the sides of her hair. With brown sandals on her feet, she was ready to go. *I don't look five-star restaurant fancy, but I look nice enough ... and I'm following the rules.*

In the living room, Jolly and Tory hooted and cat-called. She waved them off and headed to her car.

The drive to the coven house was quick, and Blake waited on the sidewalk. She wore a wine-colored halter top dress that hooked behind her neck. It was fitted at the top and waist, and had a dangerously short, flirty skirt. Once the car stopped moving, Blake slid in. "Sorry, there are too many people in the house, and I feared if you came up, they'd yank you in and we'd never leave. I ... well, I kind of want you to myself right now."

Before Maria started the car, or lost her nerve, she smiled at Blake, leaned over, and kissed her. Blake reciprocated, deepening the kiss, lifting her hands to slip them into Maria's hair. After a few moments, Maria pulled back and practically purred.

Blake smiled. "Not that I'm complaining .... As far as I'm concerned, do that whenever you want. But was there a reason for that?"

"More than one, actually." She navigated towards her favorite Thai restaurant.

"Are you going to share with the rest of class?"

A warm tingle traveled up Maria's body. *Gods above. This is what I missed on all those dates. The easy banter, and my body's reaction.* "Maybe I'll give you one, if you don't distract me while I drive."

"Am I distracting you, beautiful?" Blake's voice dropped with those words and went right to her core. It took everything in her not to moan, pull over, and climb into Blake's lap.

The car came to a stop with a jerk as she hit the brakes too hard. "Sorry. I almost missed the stop sign."

Blake laughed softly under her breath. "I guess that gives me my answer."

Keeping silent, Maria continued down another block. "No, the stop sign was blocked."

Blake turned and checked. "What? Behind that ... oh, wait, a bird flew by. So, behind the bird?"

A laugh burst out of Maria as she found a place to park. She locked the car and made her way to Blake, who pulled her into her embrace, lowering her face for a soul-shattering kiss. Moaning, Maria's hands curled up Blake's bare and silky-smooth back.

Once the kiss ended, Maria took a shaky breath and asked, "What was that for?"

"Because I like kissing you." Smiling, Blake reached down, slid her hand into Maria's, and walked with her into the restaurant.

Maria's face warmed as they entered and were seated. The place was packed, but Connie had made a reservation for them. Having a packmate who knew most of the other chefs in town could be really helpful at times.

They were given a round table in the corner, away from the rest of the people, with the chairs placed across from each other. Blake got to the table first and shifted the seats so they'd be sitting next to each other. With the size of the table, their legs would touch the whole meal ...

That won't be distracting. No, not at all.

The waitress asked if they wanted anything right away. Blake smiled at her, then Maria, saying, "I could use a Thai coffee. I don't know about you, but I love the taste, and I want to be wide awake for a few more hours."

Gulping, Maria nodded in agreement.

The waitress smiled at them. "So, two coffees?"

Maria breathed in through her nose, trying to calm her pounding heart. "Yes, please, and thank you." *Definitely not like the other dates.*

Blake reached down and squeezed Maria's knee. "Let's figure out what we want to eat."

Every muscle in Maria's body clenched. "I agree. I think I know what I want to eat, but we should start with the menu." She shut her eyes and lowered her head to hide her smile. She couldn't believe how bold she was being.

When the waitress returned, they each ordered.

Blake spoke softly. "So, when are you going to let me in about that first kiss?" Her warm hand gently rubbed up and down from Maria's knee to the hem of her skirt.

Maria slowly looked up into her piercing blue eyes. "I've heard tell, getting a first kiss out of the way makes the rest of the date easier. Less confusion about if there will be a kiss or if it'll be good."

"Hmm." Blaze leaned a bit closer. "But you see, we'd already kissed on the beach, and as far as I was concerned, I knew it was good. There's no doubt in my mind we'll be joining ... lips ... more tonight."

Taking a slow breath, Maria heard how ragged it sounded. "Okay, you may be right." Her eyes shot down to Blake's mouth and back up to her eyes—so close it took up her ...

everything. "Then maybe I just wanted to kiss you. See if it was like I remembered."

The other woman moved in a bit closer until they shared each other's breaths. "And was it? Was it like you remembered?"

Mouth dry, Maria found it hard to get words out. "No." The word was soft and airy.

"Oh?"

"It was better." She tried not to squirm admitting this to Blake, but her mind was short-circuiting, like one of her computers on the fritz.

Blake closed the distance between them for a quick brushing of their lips. "Good. We should continue to practice, see if we can keep improving."

Suddenly, Maria wished she'd worn underwear. She clenched her thighs together.

"Who had the panang chicken and the pad thai?" The waiter asked.

Maria jerked up at the waiter's words, gaping for a moment. "Um, just put the plates down and bring some empty plates. We'd like to share ... eat family style. Did you bring the green curry as well?"

He looked at the ticket. "Oh, yeah. I'll run and grab that with the plates."

Once they had plates and started to eat, Maria told Blake about building an app and website for a new company.

"That's amazing. I love that you're so technical." Blake's eyes shone as Maria spoke.

"You're not bored or annoyed by all this IT stuff?"

"Not at all."

Maria rubbed her eyes. "What if I told you—outside of Georgette, who works with me—you're one of the first people to think anything I do is interesting."

"I'd say I was gobsmacked. Like, smacked by a gob, and not the good kind either—the kind where I'd need to use my safe word."

Maria laughed loudly, and the people at the next table looked over at them. She leaned in and lowered her voice. "Do you have much use for safe words?"

"You know, I had this friend who was dating this guy. He wanted to use 'supercalifragilisticexpialidocious' as a safe word. It was going great until he started getting excited and saying, 'super' over and over. It wasn't until later that she realized he was trying to say the safe word. Needless to say, the two didn't date for very long."

Maria covered her mouth to stop herself from spitting out her coffee as she laughed. That caused Blake to laugh. The story was ridiculous. Maria choked out, "It was you, wasn't it? You were 'the friend.' This happened to you."

Blake blushed, and it was adorable. "Well, maybe."

"That's fantastic." Maria took another bite of her food. "You know, I've heard it was a pain in the ass being gay in ancient Greece."

Blake's eyes widened, and then she laughed. "Is that why olive oil became so popular?"

"Exactly!"

They both laughed. Then they focused on eating. Maria learned that Blake's friend Gretel was finally playing nice, and that her mom was in town. Hopefully, she'd come to the pack house and meet the pack. And, most intriguing of all, Blake had a new job ... she was staying in Santa Cruz!

"Can I come and visit you at work?"

Blake smirked. "Could I come watch you work some time?"

"You could, I just don't think it'd be as entertaining."

Blake sighed. "I mean, you could always strip while you code, right?"

Maria laughed. "I don't think my boss would approve. Naked coding is purely an at-home thing."

"I can get down with that." Blake wiggled her brows. "But, in all seriousness, Pendulum is a public establishment, anyone can walk in, get a table, and drink. Just realize, to get tips, I flirt with everyone."

"Are you saying you don't really like me? I'm practice for your job?" Maria gave Blake the biggest puppy-dog eyes she could muster.

Blake laughed. "I'm saying, if you come, you'll see me groping everyone and being groped. You'll also see me kissing other people, men and women. Are you okay with that?"

Maria thought about this. Blake half-naked, sashaying around a room, being the object of desire to everyone around her. Just when she didn't think she could get hotter. She licked her lips. "Did you say if I see you getting groped I'd come?"

A groan was the only warning Maria had before Blake leaned over and let her hand slide up under her skirt. Maria quickly darted a glance around the restaurant, but they were alone. When Blake's hand reached the top of her thigh, she moaned in Maria's ear. "Gods above, you really came without undies on. We need to get the check and leave ... now."

Maria leaned over and whispered in her ear, "Your place or mine?"

"Mine. Werewolf hearing is too good and I'm not wasting this slickness on waiting for another night. I want to taste you, Maria. Every inch of this amazing body." She pulled her hand back, which was good; Maria was tempted to pull Blake's dress off there and then.

They paid the bill, left a tip, and headed out. When they got to Blake's place—coven headquarters—the house was empty. Blake led her up to her room, and Maria felt exhilarated and shy.

Blake reached around Maria's neck and unbuttoned her shirt. She slowly traced down the sides of Maria's body to the bottom of the shirt and pulled it up, careful to collect the elastic of the shelf bra when she reached it. "I've been wanting to see you naked ... well, since we met. You are luscious."

She took one of Maria's nipples into her mouth and swirled her tongue around it. A sound left Maria she didn't recognize as she leaned into the warmth. She heard a clunk. Blake's other hand had unbuttoned her skirt and, suddenly, she stood bare in front of the blond goddess of a woman.

She went to cross her arms over herself, then saw the desire in the other woman's eyes as she took it all in. "Lie down on the bed."

Maria backed up as Blake stripped off her dress in one motion. She scooted up until she rested in the middle of the large bed. Blake crawled over her, her hair a waterfall tickling up Maria's body. She dipped to kiss Maria, then trailed kisses down her neck. Her tongue trailed patterns and tasted its way down.

She spent time nipping and licking each nipple. Maria's back arched up to the delightful mouth, her head falling back as her body writhed with sensations.

Then Blake continued down until she made it to Maria's clit. "I've been dreaming of spending time here. I hope you don't expect me to hurry."

Maria tried to answer, but all that came from her was a quivering moan. Her body, tingling and warm, arched up, reaching for what it wanted.

With a satisfied hum, Blake dipped her head and licked up Maria's center. Electricity shot through her. A warm hand on her lower belly held Maria in place. As Blake's tongue continued its assault, she probed inside with fingers, finding a rhythm that made time and thinking stop.

Maria's world became Blake's tongue and her fingers. Heat and tension built and her body soared, getting closer and closer. Blake scraped her teeth. "Come on, sexy wolf, howl for me."

She broke, screaming out Blake's name as the world fractured around her. Trembling with the pleasure of the orgasm, Maria collapsed boneless onto the bed. Blake crawled up to cuddle next to her, tucking Maria into the crook of her arm.

Once she could talk again, Maria sighed. "I can't move."

"Good. Then sleep."

"But what about you?"

"I quite enjoyed myself."

Maria tried to growl, but all that came out was a yawn. She curled into the other woman's side and slid her arm over her waist. They fit well together. Before she could ponder this truth further, sleep overtook her.

CHAPTER 29 - THE WAY TO WAKE UP
Blake

Blake woke up to a weight on her waist and warmth trailing down her neck. Opening her eyes, a curtain of brown waves covered her as a hot mouth nibbled down her neck.

"Hmmm," she hummed. "This is a nice way to wake up."

"I'm glad you think so, now, let me investigate the beauty below me. Your body is fantastic. Now, no distractions."

With a low chuckle, Blake rubbed her hands down Maria's back, her warm silky skin tingling her hands. When she got to the round hips, she traced her hands up the other woman's sides to her full breasts.

Maria paused above her, head hanging down, breath rough, as Blake investigated her body. She moaned and scooted lower. "Bad, Blake! This is my seduction." Her mouth landed on Blake's nipple and sucked it in. Her fingers lightly teased the other one.

Slowly lifting up, she let her tongue circle to the tip, then dipped back down, using her teeth to stimulate and play.

Blake groaned, touching any part of Maria she could get her hands onto, her shoulders, tangling her hands into the woman's hair.

Maria's mouth was magic as it continued to spend time with each breast. Then her hand dipped down to play with Blake's clit and she could stop herself as she bucked up, eyes crossing with desire.

Maria's fingers dipped lower and she hummed. "You're wet. I think you're having fun."

Blake was panting too hard to answer and Maria chuckled evilly.

She went back to sucking as her fingers continued their play.

Body buzzing, Blake thought she'd explode with joy and pleasure. As Maria played her body like an expert, she broke, orgasming.

"Well, that was fun. I wasn't even done." Maria sat back. "I wonder if I could get you to make those fun sounds again."

Blake leapt over and pinned Maria down. "You're going to kill me. How about we go get coffee ... food ... then think about our next round?"

Maria gazed up into the mesmerizing eyes above her. "Coffee ... that sounds amazing."

Climbing from the bed, Blake pulled Maria behind her. "Come on, sexy. I have some big t-shirts we can slip on."

The color drained from Maria's face. "I don't have any undies. If anyone else is here, I'll have to go without."

Blake laughed. "Come on. Coffee comes before freaking out."

"Fine."

The oversized t-shirt hit Maria's knees. "See, no flashing anyone, not even on the stairs." She seemed to relax.

Outside the bedroom, the divine scent of brewing coffee wafted up to them. Maria grumbled. "I don't know if I'm excited that the coffee is made or embarrassed."

"Be happy. I'm sure whoever is here will be."

"I am. Now come eat the feast I'm making," Mom said from the kitchen, barely speaking louder than they'd spoken. *Damn wolves and their over-sensitive hearing.*

"You could've pretended you couldn't hear us, Mom."

"What's the fun in that, sweetie?"

Rolling her eyes, she led Maria down to meet her mom.

They took seats at the island. "Hi, Blake's mom. I'm Maria." Her cheeks were a bit red with a blush. *I guess meeting my mom like this wasn't what she'd hoped for.*

"Hi, darling. You can call me Joyce. It's a pleasure to meet you. Now, eat up." She placed a plate with eggs, bacon, and hashbrowns in front of each of them then a second plate with pancakes. "Blake's always preferred to separate the savory and sweet. I'm just used to doing it this way. I hope you enjoy."

Eyes wide, Maria sighed. "This looks amazing. The only person who really knows how to cook in the house only does it once a month. Well, Tamsin can cook, but she hasn't lived at the pack house in years. She'll be back in a week or two, though. I'm drooling thinking about it ... and over this food. Gods, I love food."

Mom laughed and placed coffee in front of them both. "I like you, Maria."

"Sorry, I'm babbling. I'll just fill my mouth with food; that should shut me up." Her blush deepened.

Blake leaned over and whispered. "I could think of other things you could put in your mouth to keep it busy and not talking."

Her eyes widened and Maria swatted Blake's arm before digging into her breakfast.

CHAPTER 30 - ART IN MOTION
Maria

Maria shut the door and tried to slip up the back stairs before running into anyone.

"Maria? Is that you?" Georgette called from the front of the house.

"Give me a few minutes and I'll come talk to you." She ran up the steps and made it to her door, but her friend was there with a huge grin on her face.

"Well, look at you, doing your own walk of shame."

Maria shook her head. "I'm not ashamed. I just need a shower and—" undies, "—um, clean clothes."

Georgette's grin widened. "Have fun?"

Her cheeks heated. *I wonder if there's a possibility of my cheeks permanently changing color with the amount of blushing I've done in the last few days.* "Can I just change?"

"Sure, but then we talk." Georgette spun and headed back down the stairs.

The shower felt good. Maria reviewed her morning: a delicious breakfast and a bit more play with Blake. The siren had to work today, so Maria drove her to Pendulum before heading home. Her plan was dinner with the pack and then heading to the club to watch Blake do her thing. She knew she may end up being jealous, but it could also be hot.

Once dried off, she shuffled through her clothes until she found a black spaghetti-strapped tank top that was a bit lower cut than she was comfortable with. She figured it was appropriate for her destination. The shirt was bedazzled with black rhinestones in the shapes of flowers. It flowed over her body like silky water. Her bra straps showed, so she selected her sexiest black one with matching panties. She felt pretty secure that they wouldn't get destroyed this time.

She wore an eggplant-colored miniskirt that flared out when she spun. It belted just below her belly button and reached almost to her knees. She wasn't sure what was standard for a strip club patron, but she figured it was good enough.

Opening her door, she could hear a group talking in the kitchen. She sighed, but knew it was better to get this over with all at once. She lumbered down the steps, heading for the kitchen. Orin and Georgette were already finishing up a quick meal for an army. Plates of homemade bread, sliced beef, chicken, cheese, veggies, and condiments. A large salad sat in the center of the table surrounded by dressings, small bowls with chips, and fruit. Sitting on the counter was a tray of brownies for dessert.

Maria's stomach growled its approval. "This looks amazing."

Orin smiled. "I'm glad you think so. I decided with so many people in the house, we need to cook bigger meals."

As she stood drooling, Jolly and Timothy arrived with Rainy, Tory came in, and Georgette sat at the table. Maria helped Orin bring plates, forks, and knives over for everyone before she found her own seat. The meal was exquisite.

Once Rainy had a plate, Jolly turned to Maria. "So, why are you all gussied up?"

"Um, am I?"

A single brow shot up. "You can either answer the question or be embarrassed worse. You know it isn't going to get easier, my friend."

"Fine. I'm going out to a club tonight."

Timothy jerked his gaze from his daughter. "Alone?"

"That was the plan. I can drive there and drive back. I don't really plan on drinking a lot, not that alcohol will do much to me. It should be safe."

His eyes narrowed. "Are you meeting someone there, a new date?"

She debated what to say. Everyone at the table would know if she outright lied—a superpower of werewolves. It was one of the reasons so few wolves lied in the first place. She exhaled noisily. "I probably should've worn a regular dress and changed if I'd wanted to avoid all this." She waved her hand at the table. "Such a nosy bunch."

A few snorted and Georgette agreed. "You think?"

"Okay, fine. No, I'm not meeting anyone, not really. I'm going to the club where Blake works. That's all. I'm going to watch her in action."

A snarl came from Orin, low and guttural. "I don't like her, and you're going to go to a strip joint to watch her prance around naked? Are you insane?"

Maria opened up her mouth to answer, but Orin wasn't done.

"You'll what? Sit back and watch as she goes down on some stranger, giving lap dances, making out with them, dancing naked on the stage? Is this what you've been waiting for, Maria? I don't know that I've ever really known you."

"Enough!" Georgette snapped. "I don't know what's gotten into you, Orin, but you'll stop right now. One more word, and I'll pull dominance on you, even if it means a fight. Ever since Blake's come to town—a new wolf who needs us—you've been an utter ass." She looked at Jolly and Timothy. "Sorry." She turned back to Orin. "Until Tamsin returns, you'll keep that snake tongue of yours behind your closed lips, or you'll deal with me."

Everyone at the table gaped. Georgette had never pulled rank. Werewolves had a natural pecking order in the pack, but it never mattered in their pack. They were family above all else. However, Georgette had just stated clearly where she stood on the matter and in the pack.

Standing, Orin spun on his heel and left. His footfalls echoed through the house, ending with a slammed door.

Maria trembled in her chair. Did others feel the same?

Georgette rubbed her back. "I'll go with you. I'd love to see Blake in action; it sounds fun. Not to mention the other pretty people. Art in motion."

Jolly smiled. "I think it'd be fun too. If I didn't have a kid to watch I'd go with as well."

Timothy smiled at her. "Why don't you go? I'm here."

Bouncing, Tory said, "I'm totally in."

CHAPTER 31 - GET BIGGER TIPS, THEN MARRY HER
Blake

The bartender, a blond in a mesh top and tight jeans, finished pouring the last drink on Blake's order. The bar was crowded and her table had been waiting for too long. Blake slipped the tray up to her shoulder and winked at the woman pouring drinks.

She was cute and straight. That didn't stop her from wearing tight skimpy outfits and flirting with everyone who sat in her domain. She'd worked at Pendulum for three years and knew how to make money. She'd confessed that she was more comfortable behind the safety of the bar where none of the drunk patrons could reach her.

On her first day, Blake had spoken with her during a slow hour. She'd heard all about the woman's boyfriend and how he didn't approve of her job. He liked the money, but not the outfits or where the tips came from. The whole situation made Blake shake her head.

But what if Maria hates me working here? Would I give up this work for her? Would I give it up for anyone?

She carried the tray to the bachelor party, and placed each drink on their small table.

"Hey, sexy lady." An arm slipped around her waist. "Wanna sit on my lap? I bet I have something you'd love. It's thick, long, and hard."

She wiggled her ass in his face, the strips of her skirt allowing for flashes of skin, then straightened. "Now, I can't just be giving that away for free, even for the man of the hour. If you want more, then you'll have to talk to my boss. I can offer something that might be just as good. What if I went over to one of the tables of women, and, without even warning them, sat on one of their laps, and started making out with her? Would that be worth it to you, wedding boy?"

He made a sound deep in his throat and Blake signaled her boss with a low finger wiggle. She came to stand behind them. None of the men at the table saw her, but any transactions would now become official.

"What would it be worth, lover boy? For me to go over there ..." Blake quickly surveyed the room. Good; Maria wasn't paying attention. "... and maybe make out with that curvaceous brunette?"

He squinted, trying to see through his drunk haze. "The one with the skimpy tank top?"

"Umhmm."

The two discussed a price, and once he paid, she sashayed over to her target.

The moment Maria had walked in with the other wolves, Blake wanted to find a reason to make out with her. She'd dressed to kill, and

Blake's heart pounded faster every time her eyes traveled over the top that barely covered her assets. She hoped Maria was having a good time watching her.

Without any warning, she straddled Maria, whose eyes bugged out at the sudden attention. Bending down, she whispered, "You came into my work, now I'm going to take full advantage, sexy woman. A party of men have paid good money to watch me make out with you, and I'm going to make sure they get their money's worth."

She felt Maria's body tense, then her hands came up to stroke Blake's back as their mouths met. The kiss probably lasted longer than her boss would approve, but the men hooted and cheered. When Blake slowly walked back, several other tables stuffed money in her waistband, thanking her for the show.

She grabbed her tray and took an order from a waiting table. At the bar, L'Tisha, her boss, smirked at her. "Nice game play, Blake. You got four tables riled up by kissing one girl. You should play that card more often."

Blake blushed. "Probably. It worked better than planned."

L'Tisha narrowed her eyes. "You know the girl, don't you?"

"Yeah, she's my ... I don't know. We just started something up."

"And she's okay with all of this?"

"Yep, she knew who I was when we got together. I think she thinks this is hot ... at least, I hope she does."

"Keep her. Bring her every night, get the bigger tips, then marry her."

Blake laughed and collected a tray of drinks ready to be delivered.

CHAPTER 32 - YOU WERE MY BEST FRIEND
Maria

Everything in the living room looked good. It was clean and the clutter was contained. The kitchen needed work, but in a house with eight people, a clean kitchen, especially on a Sunday morning when everyone was home, was a pipe dream. The smell of coffee filled the room.

Maria moved to the clean, untouched dining room. Back in the living room, a collection of toys had exploded all over the place. Rainy sat in the center playing, while Jolly and Timothy sat in two couches on their phones doing ... something. *How in the hell? I cleaned in here a minute ago!*

"Um ... Jolly? Timothy? We're having guests. I just picked up in this room."

Jolly laughed. "We're having a pack wolf over. If the place is too clean, then she'll be confused. This is better; it'll make her feel like this is home."

Before Maria could argue further, there was a knock. With one last look, her shoulders slumped and she made her way to the door. She opened it to find Blake and Joyce. Smiling, she waved them in. "Sorry for the mess; Rainy is rambunctious."

Joyce came in and laughed. "Oh! You have young ones. Hi, sweet love, what's your name? How old are you?" She sat down and began playing with Rainy, ignoring the adults in the room.

Blake watched her mom. "She loves kids. It's been a while since she's had any to play with. If we don't monitor the situation, she'll be down there all day."

Timothy smiled as he watched them play. "That's fine. Rainy loves making new friends."

Maria slid her hand into Blake's. "Wanna get some coffee?"

"I'd love some."

In the kitchen, Maria poured two large mugs. They sat at the table and spent a few minutes enjoying their morning brew.

A minute later, Georgette came in, poured herself some coffee, and joined them. "Morning, Blake. I assume that's your mom in there with the Ferns. She and Rainy are having a blast together. Smart move, get in with the kids, first."

Blake laughed. "Yeah, that's my mom's devious plan. We hatched it on the way over."

Georgette nodded. "That tracks. I can see that happening."

"Mom loves kids." Blake sipped her coffee. "She used to do childcare when the coven met. She volunteered, just so she could have time with the kiddos."

"Who are you and what are you doing here?" Orin's voice cut through their conversation.

"For fuck's sake. What is his problem?" Maria whispered. She began to stand.

Georgette put a hand on her arm, stopping her. "I don't know. Tamsin can't get back here soon enough. But you don't have to solve everything. Wait, listen."

"You are the smartest girl I've met in a long time, Rainy. I can't wait until we can play again." Joyce's voice was soft as she spoke to the young girl.

"You'll play with me again, later?" Rainy sounded hopeful.

"I sure will, sweet girl."

Rainy ran past and her little feet thumped up the stairs, slowly followed by Timothy's heavier tread.

There was the sound of movement, then Joyce spoke again. "I've been part of two other packs, young man, and I don't think I've ever heard such rudeness from any wolf to another in all my years. Is this a California thing? Or is it just you?" Her voice stayed soft and conversational.

"Do you often have strangers in your pack den?"

A small feminine chuckle. "I was playing with a pack child, sitting with two pack members. I would've expected a warm welcome. You were rude because you could scent my familial connection to Blake, or tell she's here. For some reason, you've decided my daughter isn't a wolf, though you've seen her shift. You've built a wall around your heart and mind, and refuse to let the man you could be grow and evolve. From what I can see, the rest of your pack has overcome this hurdle. I hope, Orin Jax, that you can live up to your grandfather's legacy."

Maria gaped at Blake, wondering if she knew what her mom meant. Blake shrugged and shook her head back, looking equally as confused.

"My what?" The anger in his voice has morphed into a soft confusion.

"I'm going to go get some of the amazing-smelling coffee. Once you've decided my daughter and I are worthy of civility, I'd love to talk with you."

A moment later, she walked into the kitchen. Georgette pointed to the cabinet with mugs. Joyce smiled as she poured herself a large mug. When she sat, Georgette almost vibrated with her curiosity. "You know Orin's grandfather?"

Joyce smiled. "He looks exactly like his grandfather. I wasn't sure what shocked me more, his appearance or his attitude."

"But how?"

"Oh, no." Joyce said, enjoying her coffee. "I'll not tell this story without Orin being here. It will wait on him figuring this all out."

Blake grunted. "Well, there goes us learning this story. From what I know of the man and his opinion of me and witches, the story will die with you, Mom."

Joyce shook her head. "Don't speak like that, sweetie. I have confidence in him. He'll come around."

Maria squeezed Blake's hand. "I don't know. Orin's not normally like this. He's always been a good man in the past. This thing he has against witches, I've never seen it before. I think your mom is right. He'll come around and we'll learn the truth."

"Before Mom heads home?" Blake looked at her, eyebrows raised in challenge.

"I don't know, Blake. Maybe I'll stay." Everyone looked at Joyce and she smiled. "What? Wolves need family. If Blake is *finally* part of a pack, I want to experience that with her. I love my current pack, but if all of you can accept her—and me—then maybe I can relocate."

Sadness came over Maria. "I would love to have my parents back in this pack. You're right that pack is family."

Georgette's face fell. "I miss them too. They always treated me like their second daughter."

"That's why you've always been like my big sister."

Joyce shifted the mug in her hands. "Werewolves have the potential to live a bit longer than the average human, but our lives are aggressive ... tough. I'm sorry for your pain, dear."

Maria nodded. "Enough. We have too much to worry about. We're not going to look back."

Connie walked into the kitchen. "Morning, everyone. I hear someone has been picking on my husband."

Maria smiled wide, trying not to laugh. Joyce's face fell and the color drained from Blake's face.

After pouring coffee, Connie shrugged. "Unlike most of you, I don't have any of the weird werewolf closed-minded malarky. I'm assuming it's because I was bitten. You all are messed up because you were born like this." She took in Joyce and Blake's worried faces. "Now, don't worry, I added to his misery before coming down here. I'm just glad he didn't scare anyone off before I could come down and meet you."

Orin followed behind her. He hesitated at the threshold. "You knew my grandfather?" His voice was soft and uncertain.

Joyce leaned back in her chair as Connie sat. "I did."

"My parents told me he was killed by witches and no matter how good some were, we should never trust them. They loved our alpha and his family, but the fact that our last alpha, well, the last decent one, was married to a witch ... it always rubbed me wrong. At least he never tried to bring her here."

Joyce sighed. "Your grandfather was the beta of a great pack, Orin. The pack wasn't completely destroyed. The black witches tried, but other packs joined with good witches, showing everyone that when wolves and witches work together, good things can happen."

Maria gaped at her. "Are you talking about the South Dakota pack?"

"You know?" Joyce asked.

"Tamsin just told us. She's been trying to figure out what to do with a new pack member who can do magic."

Blake's jaw dropped. "She wants me?"

Georgette slapped her arm. "Or course she does. Why wouldn't she want a spectacular wolf?"

Maria shook her head. "So, Orin, you've spent your life hating witches much more than the rest of us, thinking they destroyed your family."

"Yes. Because they *did* destroy my family, and my pack. I was brought here by a pack member who survived, but I think we were the only two survivors." He looked confused and sad. "That coven ... they wiped out everyone I loved. But then, how did you know my grandfather?"

Joyce pressed her hands together in front of her face, then leaned on her hands. "Not everyone in your old pack died, Orin."

"But that's what I was told. I was told the witches killed everyone I loved and to never trust any witches. No witch should ever be trusted." His face mirrored the confusion in his voice.

Joyce moved to him, rubbing his arms. "Do you remember any of the other pack members?"

"There were twenty of us. I remember my family and a lot of adults."

"What about the other younger wolves?" Joyce asked. "Do you remember any of them?"

Orin closed his eyes. "I ... I don't know."

"I remember you, Orin. I used to watch after you, up until I left for college. We were friends."

His face scrunched up as if he was trying to think about something painful. "But everyone was killed ... it can't be you. No one survived. If they did I would've been told, wouldn't I have been? Someone would've come for me ..." He looked at his hands and then up into Blake's mom's face. "Joyce? Is it really you? I was told that you were killed first ... I cried for days because you were my best friend ... you weren't killed?"

Maria wanted to weep for the boy Orin had been. All these years living in pain because of a lie. And he'd never shared with anyone what had happened. If he had, maybe his pain could've been alleviated years ago. He could've been reconnected with old pack members, family, friends.

Joyce wrapped her arms around him and he started to cry.

CHAPTER 33 - A NEW ALPHA IN TOWN
Tamsin

Stepping from the plane, Tamsin trudged down the corridors and hallways full of people. Paige's hand on her shoulder was the only thing keeping her sane in all the crowds. She gazed back at the other woman. "It's illegal to kill other people, right?"

A middle-aged man near her snapped his head in her direction before quickly tottering off under all his bags.

Paige laughed, the sound lifting Tasmin's mood. "Yes, yes, it is." She yanked Tasmin back and gave her a quick kiss. "And the logistics and paperwork would be worse than closing up your apartment and getting the moving vans set up to move back here."

Tasmin groaned. "Don't remind me. We're not seeing our stuff for days."

"If ever," she said in a chipper voice. "But just think, if it's all lost somewhere out there, in the world, then we can just get new stuff."

"You're not helping."

"Oh, yes I am. You love me because of this."

"Or despite it."

A small tug, and their bodies were fully pressed together, and Paige's mouth demanded a deep kiss. A few people passing them grumbled at yet another obstacle in their paths.

Tamsin melted against Paige, the stress of travel seeping from her body. After her tongue completed a thorough investigation of the other woman's mouth, Paige said, "We aren't out of this mad house yet."

"No, and we're just heading to another madhouse. I love that you think our lives will ever be calm again. That was one thing Chicago had going for it. You texted Georgette, right? After we landed? She's probably waiting in a pile of cars."

Paige quickly checked her phone and nodded. "I got a reply from her. Let's get out of here, find the car, and get away from all these people. So, we'll never be alone again?"

"It'll be okay. It'll only take a few months ... years ... to get this whole pack and alpha thing figured out."

"I mean, I've been a wolf for months. I'm sure I'll get it all sorted."

Laughing, they made it out of the airport. They found Georgette's Subaru and got themselves and their luggage inside as quickly as they could.

"How was your trip?" Georgette slowly pulled into traffic.

"It was," Tamsin said.

Paige squeezed Tamsin's leg. "Don't listen to her. The flights were nicely uneventful. She's just frustrated because all her possessions are in a truck somewhere between here and there.

She wants to be with the truck, but knows we're needed here."

It took some maneuvering, but they finally made it onto the interstate. Georgette shrugged. "I'm thrilled you're home, but you could've taken a few more days. After two and a half months, a couple more days wouldn't have made that much of a difference."

Tamsin growled low in her throat.

Georgette laughed. "I mean, thank the Gods you're back, oh fearless leader. We've barely survived. I don't think we could've gone even another day without you. We're barely hanging on by a thread."

Paige leaned on Tamsin's arm, shaking with her amusement. "Oh, we're going to get along. You're fun."

"So, have you solved the problem of a witch at the pack house?"

"Oh, I didn't, but Joyce did."

"Who's Joyce? I leave for a few days, and now what's happened to the pack?" Tamsin's head began to pound. If it wasn't everyone texting her everyone's every move, then it was radio silence.

Georgette spent a few minutes explaining what had happened the previous weekend. Orin and Joyce had spent a lot of time over the subsequent week telling stories about what they remembered. They called the South Dakota alphas, who were the same as the ones who'd been around all those years ago, and a lot of healing had been done. Apparently, no one had known the Santa Cruz Orin was the same one as the kid who'd been whisked away from South Dakota.

For the first time since hearing about the new wolf, Tamsin relaxed.

When they finally got home, Tamsin and Paige shuffled to their set of rooms. Touring it, it was just as she remembered as a kid: bedroom, bathroom, office, and small private kitchen. As the alpha, she needed a bit of privacy at times, and this space provided it. She'd thought about having it remodeled while she was in Chicago, but there hadn't been time for her and Paige to figure out the design. For now, she was content to collapse on the bed and relax.

Paige stood over her and smirked. "You know the pack is waiting on us. There are new members, and old ones who missed you. You can't hide. Not yet."

"Did *you* know I don't always like you?"

"That is *not* true. Now get up."

"You could come down here, and we could ... cuddle." Tamsin tried to sound seductive, but a yawn ruined it.

"I don't think 'cuddle' is what you'd do. You'd just fall asleep. How about we just go do the thing?"

"What do I get if I get up?"

Paige put her hands on her hips. "What do you want?"

"You, naked, for an entire day."

"You know, we've been in Chicago, alone, for weeks. How about we see what responsibilities we have before we try escaping them?"

"Again, not liking you."

Paige laughed and pulled her up. "Come on, Ms. Alpha. Let's do this."

Together, they went to face their new pack.

CHAPTER 34 - ALWAYS
Blake

Maria lay beneath Blake. It was Sunday morning and Blake had barely slept. Under her, Maria bent her far leg, then wrapped it around Blake's. She reached up to push her hair behind her ears. Blake leaned down to capture Maria's mouth in a searing kiss. Tongues clashing, she lowered herself so she half covered the other woman.

When she pushed up, her hair continued to fall around them. "I want to wake up every morning just like this."

"Sounds perfect to me. Though, with my schedule, you'll be asleep most mornings when I leave. I get to take advantage, I believe." Her fingers trailed down Blake's back leaving fire in their wake.

"But which house?" Blake had finally been accepted by all the wolves. They wanted her to be part of the pack down to living at the pack house, but she was also a coven witch. She didn't want to lose that part of herself. Living at the coven house meant she could help them out with maintenance. *Admit it to yourself—it also means privacy.*

She'd never lived with a group like a werewolf pack. The closeness of all the wolves was warm and inviting, but it also got overwhelming.

Maria's hands tightened on her back, pulling her down. Once they were cuddling together on her bed, she intertwined her legs with Blake's.

Soon, Blake couldn't tell where one of them began and the other ended. She sighed happily.

After a quick kiss to Blake's shoulder, Maria snuggled even closer. "Do we have to choose? I've lived here my whole life. As more people move in, I feel more grounded. I have a feeling, until you've gotten used to it, the opposite will be true for you. So, we'll leave some clothes at both homes, and on days you need an escape, we'll stay there. It isn't like the house needs maintenance *that* often."

A tension Blake didn't even know she'd been holding relaxed. That sounded perfect. "You're amazing, Maria Sanchez."

"I'm just excited about today. Which reminds me, we should probably get dressed."

"I don't even know what to wear. Is it something formal?"

"No. I usually go with simple: a dress and flats. But jeans and a t-shirt work well, too."

"Will you go without undies so that everytime I look at you I have something good to distract me?"

Maria slapped Blake's hip. "You're incorrigible."

"That wasn't a 'no.'"

It took a bit of time, but they dragged themselves from bed and down to join the rest of the pack for lunch.

Once all the people were sitting in the dining room, the only table big enough for everyone, Tamsin cleared her throat. "The full moon is on Saturday. It would probably be better to do this then, but this ceremony can be done any time within three days of her glory. It is one of the reasons Paige and I flew back yesterday."

A cheer went up around the table. Blake watched, uncertain about what was going on.

"You've all, for the most part, bonded as a pack, but the true power of the pack hasn't blanketed over all of us yet. Some of us can sense each other, but I'd like all of it. I know the magic varies from pack to pack, alpha to alpha, but Dad could talk to us mind-to-mind in wolf form. From what I understand, my grandpa could do that as well, even in human form when it was really important. With the pack bonds in place, it can help with the bonds between all of you as well."

Blake raised her hand and Tamsin waved at her with a muttered, "You can just speak, we aren't in a classroom."

"Okay, but what if I'm not sure, or if at a later date I want to switch packs or ... I dunno, I have a lot of questions."

Mom squeezed her knee. "It's okay, love. I don't know how long I'm staying, but I'm going to participate and join. If and when I head home, I'll be able to switch back to that pack. Tamsin needs to establish her pack for herself and for us. It'll smooth a lot of things over. Give us a bit of structure. Trust me, sweetie, it'll be fine."

Paige looked up at Tamsin. "And after the ceremony, we go for a run? Like, all of us? During the daylight hours? In the middle of Santa Cruz?"

"Yes." Tamsin smiled at the intensity of her questions.

"How the hell doesn't anyone know about all of you, it makes no sense." Paige muttered.

Connie patted her back. "I know, right? I had the same questions my first time. You'll see. It's all about the magic." At the word magic she waved her hands in a rainbow gesture.

The group finished their soup and sandwiches, cleaned up, and went to the backyard.

Between the kitchen and the far wall, well away from the majority of the open area of the backyard, was a firepit. Jolly and Tamsin started a fire while everyone else took seats and watched.

When the first wouldn't light, Blake asked, "Would you like help? Every witch knows a basic lighting spell. But ... I don't want to bring anything too witchy into this if it'll be weird."

Jolly fell back on her butt. "Please, if you can get this process done faster, then help us. Lighting the fire is my least favorite part of the ritual."

Blake flicked her wrist, and a small flame started in the center of the pile of kindling. She could only light a fire about the size of a candle's flame, but with what they'd set up, it was enough to get a good blaze going.

Tamsin stood. She looked around at the faces sitting around the fire pit and a serene smile spread across her face. "We pray to Gaia, our Mother Earth, to bless our pack. We call upon the four elements, fire, air, water, and earth, to form our bond and make us strong. With fire, our pack has purpose and determination. Through air our communication is clean and clear. Water joins us, and earth lets us run free in two forms. I ask that you each take a sip of this chalice of water and pass it around."

Blake watched as each member in the circle sipped and passed the silver cup, engraved with wolves howling at the moon, filled with water. When it got to her, she took a moment, gazing down at the liquid. Her thumb traced the side, finding small gems she hadn't seen when Tamsin had held the chalice up. Maria rubbed her leg, breaking her out of her worry. She sipped and passed the water to her mom sitting on her other side.

Once the water returned to Tamsin, she finished the last of it. "I now ask that each of you speak the words, 'I choose to join the Coastal Pack.'"

Blake listened as the words buzzed around the group, one by one. Each person spoke the words clearly, smiling, happy. To them this was a celebration. Nerves still buzzed within her, but after Maria said the words she nodded at Blake.

Blake licked her dry lips, gazed around the circle at all the members staring at her, and gave a nod. "I choose to join the Coastal Pack."

A warmth infused her as a yellow haze of animal magic followed the words spoken. The pack was doing real magic. A connection between animals. Her dread began to morph into excitement. *I've never seen magic outside the coven before, this is ... spectacular.*

After Paige said the words, Tamsin smiled. "For today, until a time of your choosing, we are the Santa Cruz Coastal Pack. I am honored to lead as your alpha, to guide and protect. We are first and foremost a family. I hope you all feel that, too."

The flash of magic brightened almost like a burst of sunlight at the end of her words. *I can't believe I'm the only one seeing this, it's fantastic. I wish I could share it with Maria.* She leaned forward as if it could heat her face and fill her with its magnificence.

"We will run, in fulfillment of the earth portion of the four elements. Once we're out there, the pack bonds should settle on us. Welcome, everyone, to our new pack."

A cheer went up as everyone stood and headed to the back to shift. Before Blake could follow, Maria pulled her in for a kiss. "I'm so excited you did this with us. I wanted you to be part of our pack, part of my family."

Blake wrapped the other woman in a hug. "Always."

Find the Next Book
Campus Prowl, here
https://www.amazon.com/gp/product/B0C385C42X

Where to Find Harlowe Frost
Thanks for reading!
Find more of my books on my website:
http://hannahwillowauthor.com

You can also find me on:
Twitter: @hannahwillow217
Instagram: @hannahwillow217
Facebook Hannah Willow

About the Author

Harlowe Frost has been a teacher at both the high school and college level. Her parents instilled a love of reading from a young age. She grew up in the queer community. Her favorite genre growing up was fantasy and science fiction, that is, until she discovered urban fantasy and paranormal romance. What she never found in those books was the diversity in background, gender identity, and sexuality she saw in the people around her. She decided if she couldn't find that in what she read, then she would write it herself. This started her writing paranormal romance with a LGBTQ+ background.